The Light That Remains

The Light That Remains

Stories of War and Consequence

Michael Braswell

RESOURCE *Publications* · Eugene, Oregon

THE LIGHT THAT REMAINS
Stories of War and Consequence

Resource Publications
An Imprint of Wipf and Stock Publishers
199 W. 8th Ave., Suite 3
Eugene, OR 97401

www.wipfandstock.com

PAPERBACK ISBN: 979-8-3852-7231-0
HARDCOVER ISBN: 979-8-3852-7232-7
EBOOK ISBN: 979-8-3852-7233-4

VERSION NUMBER 02/02/26

Dedicated to
Bill Simon, Brantley DeLoatche
and all the other veterans
who have shared their stories
with me over the years.

Contents

Preface

FROM LIBERATING A NAZI Concentration Camp to remembering and reliving battles and wartime experiences in Europe, the Pacific, Vietnam, Iraq, and Afghanistan, these stories explore the experiences of those who fought as well as the ones who waited for them. Emotional, psychological and physical wounds and trauma lingered long after the fighting was over.

Friend and foe alike faced dramatic challenges testing their faith, conscience and basic humanity in time of war. Enduring the circumstances of combat and trying to adjust to a measure of post-war normalcy was a daunting task for survivors.

Based upon the recollection of veterans and additional reading and research, these stories capture a range of conflicts and consequences including GIs saving a mother and daughter in occupied Berlin about to jump to their deaths, a war-time romance reignited a life-time later, an elderly German war criminal brought to trial, and two African American GIs facing the challenges of returning home to a segregated South as well as soldiers experiencing PTSD and those who helped them through their struggles.

The Union General, William Tecumseh Sherman, captured the contrast between the ones who send men to war and the young men who do the fighting and dying.

"I am tired and sick of war. Its glory is all moonshine. It is only those who have neither fired a shot nor heard the shrieks and groans of the wounded who cry aloud for blood, more vengeance, more desolation. War is hell."

—WILLIAM T. SHERMAN, 1879

Acknowledgments

SOME OF THESE STORIES have previously been published in *Morality Stories, When Jesus Came to the Cracker Barrel, Remembering Peleliu, Story Sanctum, Mobius, and Red Dirt Forum.*

Scott Braswell is the author of "Sarah Salvation" and the primary author of "A Feast for Ghosts."

While based upon events and experiences related to war, this collection of stories should be taken as a work of fiction and the author's imagination.

1

The Light That Remains

THE TWO AND A half-ton Dodge truck rumbled toward the Russian checkpoint through swirling snow. Sergeant Higgs Cleery drove and Captain Will Simon rode shotgun. Sitting between them was Lieutenant Robbins from Army Intelligence, who allegedly spoke Russian and knew how to get them and their cargo back in one piece.

"Cap'n, you have any idea what's in those boxes and crates we just retrieved from the Russkies?"

Will Simon looked at Higgs and winked. "Can't say as I do, Sergeant. Maybe, the lieutenant here, can help us out."

Looking straight ahead, the lieutenant lit a cigarette. "It's classified, but then you two already know that."

Will took out his pipe and filled it with tobacco. "Fair point, Lieutenant. That said, after almost two years of fighting Germans, the sergeant and me would prefer not to risk unnecessary further military engagements, including with Russians—classified or not. And we still have that last checkpoint to get through before we're in the clear."

Robbins took a draw off his Lucky Strike. "Understood. Given that I do speak Russian as I have already demonstrated, as well as the fact that the Russian authorities have been notified, I don't anticipate any problems getting our cargo through the checkpoint and completing our mission."

Higgs Cleery popped a piece of chewing gum into his mouth. "Good thing I brought along a gift basket just in case your Russian isn't as clear on the way out as it was on the way in."

Lieutenant Robbins shot the sergeant a sidewise glance. "I graduated top in my language class so I wouldn't worry about it if I were you."

Higgs smiled. "A little insurance never hurts. By the way, when did you come over?"

"Six months ago, give or take a week's travel time," the lieutenant replied. "How about you?"

"Me and the Captain will have graced the European continent two years come the first of next month."

Lieutenant Robbins stubbed his cigarette out. "You must have seen a lot."

Will lit his pipe. "More than we would have liked to."

Robbins rubbed his hands together. "At least we won. At least, the war's finally over."

The Captain drew on his pipe and exhaled. "I'm not so sure about that. I'm guessing for a lot of folks it will never be over."

Higgs popped another stick of gum in his mouth. "Reminds me of a Brecht quote. I'm paraphrasing, but he wrote something to the effect that while we may have stopped the bastard who started the war, the bitch who bore him will at some point, be in heat again."

The lieutenant looked at the Sergeant. "Who the hell is Brecht?"

Will Simon shrugged. "My good friend and sergeant, Higgs Emerson Cleery, is a curious and widely read, self-taught man. He is also a fountain of knowledge, bubbling over with witticisms and insights. And to top it off, he speaks fluent German."

Higgs grinned at the confused lieutenant. "Bertolt Brecht is a German poet among other things. While I am not partial to his writing, given the war that you have concluded we won, that particular comment came to mind."

Turning on his military-issue flashlight, Robbins checked their location on the map. "We should be crossing the Spree around the next bend."

"How long do you reckon it'll take before we get back to the barracks?" Higgs queried.

The lieutenant folded the map and placed it in his jacket pocket. "Can't say for sure, but if things go okay, we should get back well before dark."

"Good to hear," the Sergeant replied.

Coming out of a hard turn, the Spree lay before them.

Will Simon rolled down his window and peered out into the gray afternoon.

"Slow down, Sergeant. The bridge doesn't look to be very wide and I can't make it out for sure, but looks like some folks are standing next to the railing."

Lieutenant Robbins strained to get a better look. "That looks to be a mighty short rail guard. What kind of people would be standing on a bridge in weather like this?"

Higgs Cleery slowed the Jimmy down to a crawl as they approached. There were four women. Two holding babies and two holding the hands of small children.

One of the women looked at the approaching truck, then stepped over the railing. Holding her infant close to her chest, she plunged into the swirling waters below. As if given a silent command, the second woman did the same.

The lieutenant shook his head and looked at Will. "Captain, I know this is a damn shame, but we need to--our priority is to keep moving and complete our mission. We have a job to do and we don't need any trouble."

Will looked at the lieutenant, then at Higgs. "Stop the truck."

"Listen Captain, this is none of our affair," Robbins began, "And we need . . ."

Higgs Cleery gave the lieutenant a sharp elbow. "You heard the captain. All you need to do is shut the hell up, unless you want to take a swim in the Spree."

Before Will and Higgs could get to the railing, the third woman scooped up her little boy, made the sign of the cross, and plunged into the currents below.

Approaching the last woman, Higgs called out, "Mutter, warte!"

Straddling the short railing, the woman hesitated. When she turned to the sound of his voice, the small girl broke free from her mother's grasp and ran to the captain. Wrapping her arms around his leg, she looked up at him. "Bitte helfen sie unns. Bitte hefen sie unns."

"She's asking . . ." Higgs started.

"No need to translate," Will replied, scooping her up in his arms.

Higgs cranked the truck and put it in gear.

The three men rode in silence, serenaded by the squeak of the windshield wipers pushing away snow.

Will Simon noticed a slight tremor in Robbins' hand as the lieutenant lit his third cigarette.

"Lieutenant, the Sergeant and I have been in worse scrapes than this. You do your part with the Russians and we'll take care of the rest."

Robbins stared straight ahead as he drew on his cigarette. "I hope you are right, Captain. I hope you are right."

"Russkie ahead," Higgs announced. "Showtime."

The Russian border guard relaxed when Higgs greeted him, pulling a half-empty bottle of vodka from his winter coat and raising it in salute.

After a cursory inspection of the crates and boxes, the Russian turned to climb down when he heard a muffled cough. And then another. Training his flashlight on the suspicious crate, he ordered whoever it was, to come out.

A small, wide-eyed girl stepped from behind her hiding place with both of her hands covering her mouth.

Frowning, the Russian climbed down and turned to the lieutenant and Higgs, his hand resting on his holstered Tokarev.

Higgs Cleery looked at Robbins. "Tell him I have another gift for him and his comrade in the guard booth."

The Russian's eyes followed the Sergeant as he pulled back the tarp covering a basket which contained six additional bottles of vodka, a bottle of cognac, two bottles of whiskey and a dozen chocolate bars. Glancing at the girl, he nodded and took the basket.

Waving them through the checkpoint, the Russian pointed at the three men, shouted something, and laughed.

Higgs shifted into second gear. "What did he say?"

The lieutenant rubbed his temple. "He said, you Americans like them young."

Higgs Cleery grunted a profanity and stepped on the gas.

"We are damn lucky," Robbins continued. "Damn lucky that he didn't call his superiors and put us in the middle of one helluva mess."

"Luck has less to do with it than you think," Higgs snorted.

Robbins fished for the cigarette pack in his jacket. "What do you mean?"

"Lieutenant, I'm beginning to wonder what you are doing in Army Intelligence? Those Russkies may be afraid of their superiors, but like most soldiers, they also resent them. More than most soldiers, they have little use for the generals and officers who ordered them to move forward in human waves to be slaughtered with little regard for their safety or survival. Poorly trained and poorly paid, what do they really care if they trade a German or two, especially a child, for vodka and cigarettes? A drink and a smoke and a bit of chocolate offer a welcome luxury, especially when tied to a relatively small risk."

Will Simon relit his pipe. "The good sergeant here is without peer when it comes to two things. Perhaps, most importantly, he is a master in anticipating a need before it actually makes itself known to others, including me. And second, Sergeant Cleery is a literal magician when it comes to scrounging up whatever a situation requires, food, alcohol, and in emergencies, ammunition and bandages."

The Captain patted Lieutenant Robbins on the knee. "And you, Lieutenant, also performed admirably, greenlighting us through Ivan's checkpoint."

"By the way, Sergeant. What are their names?"

Higgs fished in his pocket for another stick of gum. "Couldn't get much out of the mother. She looks to be in some kind of state of shock. But her daughter let me know right away that her mother was Eva and she was Else."

Will Simon looked at the snow outside. "No doubt, they've been through a lot."

Higgs popped the fresh piece of Juicy Fruit into his mouth. "I once read an old German proverb that said something to the effect that war leaves a country with three armies. Armies of cripples, mourners and thieves."

The old coal stove began to spread its warmth into the modest two rooms that passed for an apartment in the corner of a bombed-out building that had remained for the most part, intact.

Will Simon and Higgs Cleery sat on a faded, worn-out settee with their feet propped up on a small wooden bench in front of the stove.

"I got a medic friend of mine over at the hospital to take a look at them."

Will uncorked a bottle of Kentucky bourbon. "What's the verdict?"

The Sergeant leaned closer to the fire, warming his hands. "The mother has been through it. Some cuts, bruises and signs of . . . The 'doc' said there's no visible signs of venereal disease. But you never know, not this early."

"And the girl?"

"Momma must have done good in protecting her daughter," the sergeant sighed. "No sign of abuse."

After washing and putting on some ill-fitting clean clothes, Eva and Else ate the soup Higgs had warmed on the stove. Exhausted, they bedded down on a pallet in the corner.

Will poured whiskey into the sergeant's cup. "Higgs, you have come through again. I don't know how you do it."

Raising a cup to his Sergeant, he smiled. "Maybe, I don't want to know how you do it."

Higgs threw back his whiskey and held his cup out for a refill. "I suppose it's a skill I acquired growing up poor and living a hardscrabble life. Maybe more importantly, my mother who was a washer woman, pushed me into reading and learning and being curious about things. When my father died, we were on our own, just the two of us. All she ever talked about was wanting a better life for me though I'm not so sure this war would qualify."

The Captain sipped his whiskey. "Your mother sounds like quite a woman. By the way, how did you find this apartment, clothes for the mother and her daughter and especially, that coal stove?"

Higgs Cleery rubbed his eyes and yawned. "Well, I do speak a little German so I got to know one of the mayor's assistants and a couple of other locals with some pull. I guess you could say, we do what we can to help each other out."

Will looked at the dancing flames. "I don't guess they feel so much like a super race trying to survive in what's left of Berlin."

The Sergeant pulled on his boots. "No doubt about that. When karma comes calling, there's gonna be some kind of hell to pay. That said, I have found no matter the time or place, most folks in most situations don't pay enough attention to what their leaders are promising them and even less attention thinking about what those promises are going to cost them."

Will threw another lump of coal into the fire. "The herd grazes while the leaders get the branding irons ready."

Rising, Higgs massaged his right knee. "Captain, I do believe you've got a bit of philosopher in you. You want me to stay the night?"

"No, I'll stay. You take the Jeep back to the barracks and get some rest. We'll figure things out tomorrow."

Opening the door to leave, the Sergeant turned and said, "Don't forget the meeting with Major Laney tomorrow at 0900 hours."

Still watching the fire, Will raised his cup. "Will do."

Will Simon looked at the two bodies huddled together on the pallet. Eva snored, waking from time to time with a jolt before getting her bearings and returning to the comfort of a restless sleep. Else snuggled against her mother in silent repose.

He poured himself the last of the whiskey and leaned back against the settee. Pulling up the wool blanket, he closed his eyes and wondered about the broken world he was a part of. He wondered how he and Higgs had ever managed to survive when so many had not? He wondered how his folks were doing back home? Was there enough rain for the crops to come in? Would he ever be able to get back to some sense of normal? He thought of fall in the mountains, the colors and smells, as sleep overtook him.

There was a weight on him. Was he dreaming? Will Simon reached for his 45. Slowly opening his eyes, he looked down to find Else asleep, huddled on the floor next to him. Her arms were wrapped around his leg, her head resting against his knee.

Picking her up, he cradled the wisp of a girl in his lap and pulled the wool blanket around her. Will thought of his grandmother. He wished he had her rocking chair.

He looked down at the four-year-old bundle sleeping peacefully in his arms. He stroked Else's tousled blond hair. God, he was tired—the kind of weariness that settled deep into one's bones. He was still above ground, but knew a secret part of himself would always remain buried with those he had left behind.

Although the war had ended, living each day with death hiding nearby had left him with a kind of emptiness. The jitters were still there, footsteps approaching, whispers in the next room, or the backfire of a truck transport, brought his senses to full attention.

The ache of experiencing something beyond description, made any possible future suspect. Still, here he was, sitting in a remnant of a bombed-out apartment with a small girl and her mother.

Else turned in her sleep, grasping his forefinger with her tiny hand.

Will stared down at what the moment offered him, innocence in the midst of war's ruin.

He touched her face and slowly exhaled.

2

Remembering Peleliu

HARRIS CAULEY SAT ON his front screened porch drinking strong sweet tea. A crow squawked its complaint from a tall Yellow Pine. He looked down at the writing pad cradled in his lap wondering if he was up to the task before him. Wiley's grandson, Will, had written him a letter requesting an account of his grandfather's war-time experience—something to remember him by. Harris and Wiley had been best friends along with "Country", a mountain of a man from Arkansas. As the saying went down south, the three of them were "thicker than thieves." They survived Guadalcanal and other battles, but only one of them made it off Peleliu alive. Here he sat with pencil and pad thinking about opening a door he had tried to keep closed for the last 40 years. Harris took a sip of tea and pressed the cold glass to his forehead. South Georgia late after-noons were still hot. Screen porches and shade trees helped, but the heat and humidity like his memories, seeped through every crack and crevice. He doodled on the sheet of paper in front of him. His VA counselor thought it would be a good idea to put things down in writing. She said something about it being cathartic—helping him to get it out of his system and finding some peace. And there was Will, a young man wanting to know more about a grandfather he never got to know who was killed at about the same age his grandson was.

Nobody understands the killing and dying of war except those who have done it and come out the other side half alive. The folks at the VFW Club who liked to bluster on about the war and the fighting that took place were impostors in Harris's mind. The real combat veterans tended to drink more and talk less. They wanted to forget what the imposters pretended to remember. Conversation between combat veterans was unnecessary. One look said it all—the haunted look of one who had returned in body, but not entirely in mind and soul. Had it not been for Harris's granddaddy, he might not have returned at all.

Granddaddy Cauley was a WWI veteran who had served in France. Harris could remember like it was yesterday when his granddaddy took him to his special place back in the hills, the place his granddaddy would go when he felt one of his "spells" coming on.

His calloused hands pulled a plug of Bull Durham tobacco out of his overall pocket. He cut a wedge off with what was left of his Barlow knife and popped it into his mouth. He leaned against an ancient oak and looked at his grandson. "Harris, you've seen things a man shouldn't see . . . probably done some things, too . . . things you'll carry with you to your grave. Same was true for me in the first War. War wears on a man. If he makes it back, he comes home an old man in a young man's body. He feels like one of them scary critters you see in the movies. . .like he doesn't belong in regular folks' world . . . like they're talking a language he doesn't understand anymore."

Granddaddy Cauley reached out and put his hand on his grandson's shoulder. "It gets better, son. Over time, it gets more tolerable. The memories will come back to you for a visit, but they don't stay as long."

The old man turned his head to one side and spit a stream of tobacco juice. "Don't know what them VA counselors call it, but when I felt a "spell" coming on, I would come up here for a couple of days, partly to be by myself and get it out of my system and partly to spare my family what was coming."

"What would you do up here?" Harris replied, rubbing his eyes.

"Well hell, Harris, I'd do all kinds of things. Sometimes, I'd build me a fire and stare at it for hours. Of course, I'd also bring along some provisions and a jug of moonshine and my shotgun. One time I painted my face in war paint and ran naked through these hills howling like a wolf. I couldn't stop a spell from happening, but I could plan around it . . . try to keep it to myself and away from my family."

"Did you ever think about shooting yourself?"

Harris's grandfather looked away and grew quiet for a moment. "Yes, I did."

"What stopped you?"

The old man spit again. "Your grandmama, your daddy and his sister. Ending it might have brought me some relief, but I couldn't put that kind of burden on them. Besides, it seemed like the coward's way out and I couldn't say for sure that shooting myself would end it. Who knows what's on the other side."

He motioned to Harris. "Come take a look at this tree I'm leaning against and tell me what you see?"

Harris peered at the old oak. "Looks like a bunch of marks from a knife blade."

"That's right. I called it my 'stabbing tree.' Sometimes in the middle of the night I'd wake up in a fury, fighting for my life. Other times, a rage would overtake me right out of the blue. Whenever that happened, I would take my knife to the stabbing tree until the killing fever passed."

The old man patted his grandson on his cheek. "This make any sense to you?"

"Yes sir, it does."

His grandfather smiled. "Well then, I'm passing my special place onto you."

Crumpling the piece of writing paper, Harris threw it on the floor and scribbled "Remembering Peleliu" at the top of a new page. Trouble was, whenever he thought about Wiley or Peleliu, a wave of sorrow washed over him that made him want to reach for the bottle. Harris used to joke with Ed Smith down at the VFW that his therapist, "Dr. Jack Daniels", had helped him over many a rough spot since the war. Of course, like most such pronouncements that was only partly true. Drinking had numbed the nightmares and pushed his memories away from the surface of his consciousness, but they had also brought grief on more than one occasion to Annie, his long-suffering wife.

"You want some more tea?" Annie shouted from the kitchen.

"No thanks," Harris replied, staring at the title he had just written and thinking a visit from "Dr. Jack" might be order before the evening was over.

"Here goes," he muttered to himself. "Time to jump off the cliff into the deep end."

A lot of people look at islands in the Pacific as tourist destinations. Azure blue water, sport fishing, diving the coral reefs and such. But for me and your granddaddy and the other Marines of the 51st regiment, it wasn't a tourist spot—it was more like a place of fire and brimstone—like the end of the world.

We had already survived several big fights, including Guadalcanal. While the previous battles had taken a lot out of us, we had prevailed. For Peleliu, General Rupertus, expected more of the same. We would engage the enemy and when the fighting went south for them, they would fight to the death with Banzai charges, the honorable way to die for the Emperor. Old Rupertus even put out the word that he expected Peleliu to be done within 4 or 5 days. Problem was, the Japs had learned a thing or two, including the futility of Banzai charges. Unbeknownst to us, they had fortified hundreds of caves with mortars, 20 mm cannons, 47mm guns and even some anti-aircraft artillery. They dug out an endless maze of tunnels to move troops and weapons to wherever they wanted to make a stand. When our regiment moved ashore on the northern end of the landing area, we faced what amounted to a giant coral pillbox overlooking our part of the beach with plenty of firepower.

Me and your granddaddy, Wiley, and the rest of our regiment under Colonel Chesty Puller were supposed to push north toward Umurbrogol, more a collection of hills than a real mountain. When the LVTs brought us in, things went from bad to worse. The Japs caught us in a crossfire. Before we knew it, they had taken out 60 of our landing craft. I saw one LVT blow up in a ball of flame. It was 100 degrees or more—felt like 200—like we were fighting in a damn furnace. Sounded like the 4th of July except the fireworks were all aimed at us.

When we came in on those LVTs, we caught hell. Most of us veterans were either silent or cussing up a storm, but the new troops—that was another matter. They were praying or puking their guts out or doing both at the same time. I saw one poor kid praying with tears streaming down his face. I think his name was Johnny. He was dropped before he got to shore.

Our LVT was hit by a 47 mm round so we had to wade through a coral reef while the Japanese machine gunners had a field day raking us over the coals.

Annie stuck her head out of the sliding glass door. "Honey, you about ready for supper?"

Harris stopped writing and looked at his wife. "Tell you what. Just bring me a tomato sandwich and put on a pot of coffee if you don't mind."

Harris listened to the crickets signaling the onset of evening as he drifted to a place he had never quite left.

At the end of the first day, we still felt like sitting ducks. We held our stretch of the beachhead, but that was about it. More than a thousand of our boys were killed or wounded. Firing from the slits in that Pillbox and mortars from those caves, we had seen very few Jap soldiers. What we did see was plenty of hot lead and dead Marines.

Word came down that General Rupertus still thought the Japs would soon fold. Me and Wiley and "Country" weren't buying it. Looking at maps, listening to Intel and planning strategies at HQ was one thing, but we had seen enough combat to know that Rupertus like most generals was full of it. Now our Colonel, Chesty Puller, he was different. We would follow him into hell, which is what I guess we did. Colonel Puller was one of us.

The Japs held the high ground on top of the "Point" where that Pillbox was located. Their heavy machine guns and artillery pretty much kept us pinned down and caused a lot of casualties.

Chesty Puller finally had enough. He ordered our Captain, George Hunt, to capture the "Point." So off we went, short on supplies and minus the machine guns we had lost in the landing. We got pinned down right away and the Japs punched a hole in our line and near about surrounded us. One of the rifle platoons started taking out Japanese gun placements with grenades and close quarters fighting before a 47mm gun placement in a lime-stone cave stopped them in their tracks. That's when the Captain and Corporal Henry Hahn bellied up to the cave and Henry fired a rifle grenade through an opening. When he did that, the whole damn place exploded. The Japs came running out of the cave—they looked like Roman Candles going off. We shot 'em all. I guess in hindsight it was the merciful thing to do with them being on fire and all, but mercy wasn't on our minds. We would have probably shot them even if they weren't on fire. We finally did capture the "Point", but K Company got no rest. Our reward was more than a day's worth of counter attacks. It felt like we were fighting off the whole Japanese army. We were damn near out of supplies and ended up fighting hand to hand—kill or be killed. Wiley killed five Japs with his trenching tool and "Country" killed three more with his homemade hunting knife. Scalped the one who stabbed him through his thigh with a bayonet. Needless to say, it wasn't a pretty sight.

When it was over, there were 18 of us Marines, more or less, still standing. Captain Hunt and Corporal Hahn were later award-ed the Navy Cross which was well deserved. Our reward was hot food and some rest.

Harris's hand shook as he poured himself a glass of whiskey. The pot of coffee was long gone.

"Harris, it's late. Don't you think . . ." The look in her husband's eye stopped Annie in mid-sentence. She had seen it before—the tense face and hollow, empty eyes looking backwards into an uneasy past.

Her husband's face relaxed a bit. "Another pot of coffee would be good—make it strong."

Harris squeezed his wife's hand. "I've got to finish this thing. I'm afraid if I stop, I won't be able to continue. I'm tired of going down the 'rabbit hole'. I . . . I need to keep going for Wiley and his grandson and for . . . I don't know. All I know is that I need to keep going."

In the tropics, night falls fast and when it gets dark, it gets black as the Ace of Spades. Night fell quickly at Peleliu. Day was better than night. It was all hell on earth, but still, day was better than night. At night, the Japs would infiltrate our lines and crawl into our foxholes. We had two-man foxholes, but . . .

Harris began to cry. He bent over, his body wracked with sobs. Annie came to the door, but said nothing. She had seen it all before. All she could do was wait until it passed. After drinking two cups of strong coffee, Harris re-entered the 'rabbit hole.'

That's when Wiley, your granddaddy, saved my ass. It was my turn to keep watch, but I fell asleep. A Jap jumped me and Wiley jumped him. While Wiley was taking care of him, another one bayoneted your granddaddy in the back. I finished both of them off with my Kabar and hollered for a Medic. By the time help came, Wiley was gone. I did what I could for him and held him in my arms as he drew his last breath. He didn't say anything . . . just looked at me. I could tell by his look that he didn't blame me . . . we were closer than brothers . . . still, I guess I blamed myself.

Harris stopped writing. With his head in his hands, he remained silent, rocking back and forth. Finally he sighed and picked up the writing pad.

We had it bad on the "Point," but for the life of me, I don't know how any of the boys on "Bloody Nose Ridge" made it out alive. The 1st Battalion had over 70 percent casualties in six days of fighting. The paths between the coral ridges were narrow. Our boys were constantly trapped in a lethal crossfire. The going was slow and the casualties were high, then the Japanese snipers started picking off our medics and stretcher-bearers.

What Everett Pope and his Company did at "Bloody Nose Ridge" is still to my mind, impossible. Against all odds, he and his company of Marines fought through the swamp to take Hill 100. When he and the 90 remaining Marines finally seized the crest of the hill, they found themselves not at the top, but at the base of yet, another hill. The Japs commenced to pound them with machine guns, mortars and rifle fire.

When night fell, the bastards came at them again. At first light, only Pope and seven of his men were still alive. Bodies were everywhere. Captain Pope was also awarded the "Medal of Honor," but I don't imagine it counted for much against what he lost.

Harris sat for a long time listening to the sounds of a hot, summer night—trying to reign in his emotions and collect his thoughts. Finally, he reached for the bottle of whiskey, but instead poured himself another cup of coffee.

As I look back on it all, we were fighting an enemy who were taught death was an honor. I'm sure some of the Japs were scared like us—maybe a lot of them, but for many, surrender was unacceptable. Like the NAZIS, they thought they were a superior race and everybody else was beneath them. No doubt they had good and bad like we did, but when push came to shove and they knew they were losing the war, they didn't think much about surviving, about what happened next after the war. I don't guess they could bear the thought. They were more about dying than living . . . and killing all of us they could.

What they did to some of our wounded—cutting their hands off and mutilating their bodies—showed me that they had turned into something not human and they near about turned me into the same thing.

It wasn't just what they did or we did. It was the war itself. We all wanted to live, but as time went on, didn't really expect to. It was like our humanity had been sucked out of us. We didn't wash or shave. Our days were spent hacking out foxholes, running for cover, hugging the ground and crawling forward all the while trying to kill the ones who were trying to kill us. I shot at anything that moved. Toward the end I even quit writing letters. Why write to a place I wouldn't be returning to or didn't belong anymore? After Wiley died and "Country" was shipped to Honolulu to recover from a head wound, I didn't get close to anyone else. I stayed to myself. Then the war ended and I was shipped home. Nobody understood, but my granddaddy and a couple of other veterans I drank with at the VFW.

Before I shipped out, I met a Navy man from a Liberty ship. His name was Joe—no Bill, Bill Simon. He handed me a crumpled piece of paper the last time we met. I read it on the ship. It was about Peleliu. I'm not ashamed to say that me and the Marines I shared it with cried when we read it. Wiley, I'm ending this account of Peleliu and your granddaddy with Bill Simon's poem. It seems fitting.

THE DEAD OF PELELIU SPEAK

On Peleliu no poppies grow, between the crosses row on row,
But only coral, rock and sand. Each cross a muted sentry, stands.
A guardian of those hallowed sands that drank our blood.
On Peleliu we fought and died.
We're restless lying side by side,
who gave our all. And now we wait,
too worn to rest, too tired to hate.
We are the earth's repatriate,
who crave long peace.

On Peleliu in coral sand, we lie and wait our sleep disturbed.
Have we, like others, died in vain, and shall we have to rise again
and hear once more the wild refrain
of bursting shell?
Oh the dread to hear us rise again, to fight on earth, in skies again,
nor listen full of fear and dread,
to footsteps of the marching dead.
Remember promises you said!
We restless lie.
Make well the peace, oh men of state,
for we the dead were taught to hate.
We learned to hate and do it well,
and make of life a living hell for those who break our sleeping spell.
So falter not.
But bring the peace of God to man!
Here us who lie beneath the sand,
white sand and damp with morning dew.
We cannot but remember you,
We men who died on Peleliu.
Oh let us sleep.

Harris Cauley leaned back in his chair. A rooster crowed in the beginning of a new day. He rubbed the cramp out of his writing hand wondered if he would now be able to find a little peace. He hoped so.

3

Bougainville Dreams

IT WAS UNUSUALLY COOL for late summer in North Carolina. George turned off the remote and stoked the fire in the hearth. "I can't believe Mickelson didn't make the cut. He's hot one week and cold the next. Looks like he's fading a bit."

Roy Wilson rose from his chair and chuckled, "Like you and me, George, like you and me."

George laughed at the thought of it. "Not that much. Still, we're hanging in there. Last week, I shot my age. That 84 felt right good."

Roy poured himself another Scotch and Soda and smiled. "That you did, my friend and as I recall, you relieved me of a crisp new five-dollar bill on that auspicious occasion."

"Roy, I've noticed that pretty much all your five-dollar bills are crisp. Most of them seem to stay put in your wallet," George replied.

Roy grinned. "You realize that's like the pot calling the kettle black."

Both men laughed.

"You want me to freshen up your Vodka and Tonic while I'm up?"

"I'd be much obliged," George responded, handing his friend a half-empty glass. "Looks like we'll be wearing sweaters at the golf tournament tomorrow."

Roy handed George his drink and settled into his 30 year-old Lazy Boy recliner. "Yep, it will definitely be chilly tomorrow."

The two old friends watched the crackling fire and sipped their drinks in silence.

"Veterans of foreign wars," George said as much to himself as to Roy. "A lot of those veterans never made it back."

Roy looked at his scarred hands. "Amen, brother. Truer words were never spoken. I look at my hands every day and thank the good Lord for sparing me. Every time my "shrapnel knee" hurts, it reminds me that I'm alive."

George stirred his drink with his finger. "I still think about the war every now and then, especially Bougainville."

"Think about it! Hell, I dream about Guadalcanal and every other damn battle I survived."

George leaned back on the sofa and looked at his friend. "It was tough enough being an Ensign and a Navigator on a Destroyer trying to intercept Japanese supply ships and convoys. I can't imagine what you boys went through."

The muscles in Roy's jaw clenched. "'43 was a helluva year. Rumor had it that Bougainville wouldn't be as hard as some of the other islands, but as usual, the military intelligence boys had their heads up their asses."

Roy leaned forward in his recliner. "The Japs had all kinds of bunkers in the jungle above the beaches and the heavy surf and steep slopes played hell with our landing. I remember you telling me about picking up some of our boys who got sideways with the landing. I'm trying to remember the name of your ship."

"U.S.S. Lardner," George replied, staring into the fire. "That is a night I will never forget. At 10 p.m., we were ordered to drop out of patrol and proceed to Bougainville to pick-up some Marines who were in distress. I heard they got ambushed in a crossfire. The coral reefs kept us from getting in too close, so those poor fellows had to try to get to us."

George took a long pull on his drink. "I've never seen anything like it. Every one of our boys were wounded. The Japs were pouring fire down on them and they were trying to fight back while swimming and paddling toward the ship. Several wounded Marines were in a skiff trying to make it . . ."

George's voice cracked as he continued. "I've never seen men so terrified. When I looked into their eyes, I saw a wildness that was more animal than human."

He drained the last of his drink. "When we pulled the last of the Marines on board, most of them couldn't even speak. One boy—a big Polish kid—had most of his right leg shot off. I've never seen so much blood. We had to burn the blankets. The stains couldn't be washed out. Two of the wounded didn't even make it back to the hospital. We buried them at sea. Only a few of those boys made it out alive."

The two old friends settled into an uneasy silence. Finally, Roy spoke. "No doubt about it, like that Civil War Yankee general said, 'War is hell.'"

The fire crackled and popped as Roy cleared his throat.

"Hill 700 was the worst it. When Bougainville finds its way into my dreams, it's always about Hill 700. The 3rd Marine and 37th Infantry had to protect the airfield. We were spread thin and the Japs attacked at night in the fog and the rain. It doesn't get any worse than that. All night long they scuttled and jabbered about, shooting off firecrackers and the like to get us to use up our ammo. In the early morning, they came in waves, hollering and screaming. We threw everything we had at them—BAR's, fragmentation grenades, rocket launchers, flame throwers and dynamite. There were a lot of heroes that day, mostly dead ones."

The weekend weather was perfect for a golf tournament—cool and clear. George was paired with Mitch McGinnis, a senior golfer from Michigan. After a quick sausage biscuit and cup of coffee, they got into their golf cart and headed toward the assigned tee box to get ready for a shotgun start. While making their way along the cart path, Mitch turned to George, "What did you do in the war?"

Waiting on several golf carts to move out of his way, George smiled at his partner, "I was an Ensign on the U.S.S. Lardner."

Mitch McGinnis looked stunned. He began to shake and moan.

George pulled the cart off to the side of the path. "Are you alright?"

Tears streamed down Mitch McGinnis's face. "I was at Bougainville. Your ship was an angel . . . ship. You saved our lives. You saved my life."

He wrapped his arms around George and sobbed. "Thank you. Thank you. Thank you."

When the golf tournament was finished, Mitch insisted on buying George a round of drinks at the clubhouse. That round led to another round, then another. They drank to their own good fortune, to their families, to the good old U.S. of A. and to the uneasy truce their emotions had made with the war and all those who hadn't made it home.

That night George drifted off into a fitful sleep to a place he didn't want to be. It was dark. Torpedoes from a Japanese submarine had found their mark on the U.S.S. Lardner. He was in a life raft paddling for all he was worth. There were three other men in the raft with him.

George shouted to the man on his right, "We've got to get clear of the ship before the magazine explodes."

Twenty yards further and the ship blew, raining fire and debris everywhere. Cries for help from wounded and drowning seamen echoed through the sounds of the dying ship.

As flaming remnants splashed and hissed around the raft, George called out for the men to paddle harder. He looked to his left and was startled to see the Polish kid paddling with his left hand and keeping the tourniquet tight on the bloody stump of what remained of his leg with his right.

The kid scowled at George. "Don't worry about me. You do your part and I'll do mine."

The four men paddled through the night until they collapsed in exhaustion. The burning ship had disappeared beneath the waves and the sea was silent. One of George's raft mates touched his shoulder. "Name's Mitch McGinnis. Looks like you're the only officer in this here raft so that makes you in charge. What do you reckon our prospects are?"

George shrugged, "Don't know for sure. Our best hope is that we'll be picked up by one of our ships come daylight."

The first streaks of dawn crept across the sky as the four weary men tried to preserve what was left of their strength.

Mitch McGinnis grabbed George's arm. "Did you hear that?"

"Hear what?"

Mitch pointed at the distant horizon. "Sounds like a boat."

Sure enough, George could hear it. He cupped his hands over his eyes and could make out the small shape of a boat growing larger as it approached the raft.

The four survivors cheered. The boat came closer and the cheers were replaced by gasps and groans. It flew the flag of the "rising sun."

"George, are you alright?"

George rubbed his eyes and looked up at his wife. She placed a hand on his forehead. "You're drenched in sweat. Should I call Dr. Stephens?"

George shook his head. "I'll be okay. Just give me a few minutes."

After a hot shower, he poured himself a cup of coffee and walked out onto the back deck of his house. He looked at the sun rising over the tree line, signaling the beginning of another day and whispered, "Thank you."

4

A Feast for Ghosts

EIN GEISTERFEST.

Captain Barris Ember stared at the words etched into the wet wood of an abandoned shed's door.

The crunch of familiar steps–quick, elongated strides–grew louder behind him and came to a stop. The footsteps belonged to Sergeant Luther, a tall, soft-spoken man with narrow shoulders and a close-cropped head of prematurely grey hair that earned him the nickname of Goat. The Sergeant was a finder of things whether a spare part for a jeep or a bottle of cognac. He had an intuitive knack for successfully searching the cracks and crevices of army life for whatever was needed at a given moment.

"Have you ever seen gray like this?" He asked in Barris's direction. "Everything–the skies, the buildings, the mud on our boots, even the air we breathe. All gray."

Barris nodded absently and took off his helmet.

"What does that say," he asked, pointing at the words scrawled across the shed wall.

"A feast for ghosts."

Barris ran his hand through his hair and turned to look at the Sargent, then turned back to the small building.

"Is that what it means?"

"Yeah, in so many words."

"Let's take a look."

The two men opened the door and walked inside.

Scratched and scrawled on the walls in no particular order were hundreds of names.

"What do you make of it, Sarge?"

"Looks like some kind of shrine," Luther replied, peering closer at the names. "'Whole families are listed, some with the ages of their children."

The Sergeant put his hands in his pocket.

"Like a wall of remembrance."

"Yeah, Captain, like a wall of remembrance."

The two men walked back outside and Sergeant Luther quietly closed the door to the small building. Barris Embers took a pack of Camels from his jacket pocket and tapped it on the back of his hand. Lighting one, he exhaled a plume of smoke and looked at the faces staring at him through the barracks fence.

His mind wandered for a moment as he looked at the camp inmates or what was left of them. They were gray too. Like ghosts, they seemed to float, their translucent skin clinging to brittle bones. The only flicker of life was in their eyes set deep in hollows of sunken faces. A community of ghosts, a band of living dead, unable to let go of the scrap-heat that had come to be their existence.

Barris Embers tossed the remnants of his cigarette to the ground.

"Hell."

"What did you say, Captain," Sergeant queried as he blew his nose on a handkerchief.

"Let's get some hot coffee."

The two men sipped cups of well-cooked coffee in the small office, listening to the rain that had begun falling.

Barris propped his feet on the tiny desk and leaned back in his chair.

"When I was a boy growing up, my grandmother had a small farm. All dust and wood really. Not much livestock, mostly chickens. I used to lay awake at night imagining them having conversations with each other—like people. Dozens of them packed together in the henhouse, stinking, noisy, and the like. I would imagine their chatter with whispers in between, They'd say, "Who's next, who's next?" to one another.

And the following morning, my grandmother would march right out there and pick one, and wring its neck. Just like that. Swift and deadly. Just about every day it would happen. What got me the most wasn't her killing the chicken, but the quick silence of the other chickens and the nervous chatter that followed. All those chickens. Each one waiting its turn."

"It was heavy. Like this place."

"When I walk around here and think about all that's happened. The bodies—all bones and gray eyes," Barris' voice wavered then trailed off, trading places with the rain's rhythm.

"Every time I walk around here, I can hear those whispers."

Luther pulled his chair closer to the little stove that popped and cracked its warmth while Barris lit a fresh Camel and continued.

"North Alabama had its gray days too in weather and disappointments. But most days were good ones . . . days worth remembering and returning to. Not like this place, thick with things best left alone. But they won't be. Hell, they can't be. There will be trials about the crimes done here. Justice comes best from when things are seen in black and white. How do you get justice from this mess? If every guard and officer who ever worked here or anywhere else such deeds were done were hung, justice would still be a question mark.

And there's the smell. A man can adjust to seeing gray even when it's thick as pea soup. Smelling it is something else. Gets in the skin and hair. Ain't never been a smell like this. Stench everywhere–in the coffee, rations–even the taste of a cigarette. Closest thing I can compare it to back home is a busted cesspool or three-day-old road kill. Only thing missing is buzzards circling above."

Sergeant Luther leaned toward the warmth of the stove and coughed. Clearing his throat, he turned toward the Captain.

"Do you know Camus?"

"Camus?"

"Yeah, Camus."

"Give me a first name."

"First name, Albert."

"Is he some kind of magician" Barris asked, lighting another cigarette off the butt of the one he had just finished.

"No, he's a writer, philosopher and poet. He said within each of us there lives an Invincible Summer, a kind of personal haven, a reservoir for peace and strength. A place to go and never be broken down."

"Sounds like a magician to me," Barris replied.

A short round of laughter erupted from both men, a kind of full-throated chuckle. The wood rafters creaked in harmony. The two soldiers recognized how nice it was to hear laughter again and both paused to recognize the oddness of the moment.

"Maybe so, maybe so," said Luther, grinning at the thought of it. "It works though—for me at least. It works enough."

"To each his own, Sarge. If your magician does the trick, I say 'hallelujah and a shot of whiskey to chase it down.' I heard that somewhere." Barris smiled as much to himself as to Sergeant Luther and blew a smoke ring toward the ceiling.

"My magician is this stove, and right now it's my hand's best friend, and if my hand is warm and happy, I'm happy, and if I'm happy, my soldiers are happy. Life's a funny thing like that. The little things connected. Little to big and big to little. There's something for your magic man to think about—what's his name? Cam . . . Camel?"

"Camus."

Barris stared at the stove, his thoughts a million miles away, slipping through the rust and wood cracks of old chicken sheds, where whispers decorate the night and wait for dawn to answer "who's next."

The next day was like the day before and the day before that. Barris finished the last of his paperwork. He stretched, massaging the soreness in his lower back. The rain had stopped for the moment. A faint ray of light found its way through the gray skies and illuminated the dingy office window. Barris looked at his watch. It wouldn't be long until evening chow.

Sergeant Luther bustled into the office.

"What's up Sarge?"

Pouring himself a cup of coffee from the pot sitting atop the stove, Luther took a long swallow.

"Looks like some kraut lieutenant's gone off his rocker down at pit one. 'Least that's what his Major just told me. Guess we need to take him down there with us along with a couple of MPs in case there's trouble."

"You shouldn't have, Martin. But I must say it's lovely. And my favorite color."

"I wanted to get you something special on your birthday. The red scarf caught my eye. I thought you would like it."

"Like it? Of course, I do. You're such a good son, Martin."

Martin looked pleased then sad.

"I wish Father were here."

"I know. I miss him too. He so loved his garden."

"He died in France."

"Yes. It was terrible, but he was brave."

"Mother, I didn't really want to enlist, but I felt . . . well, my friends and some of yours expected me to . . . you know."

"I know, Martin. It was a matter of honor. So many have lost loved ones. I'm just glad you're safe here with me now."

"Yes, I can hardly believe it. After I was wounded, they sent me here for light duty. I didn't want to come."

She smiled at her son. "Sometimes fate has its own plans. I've been waiting for you and now, my dear, you are finally here."

Martin gently stroked his mother's face and wrapped the red, woolen scarf snugly around her neck.

"I don't want you to catch cold."

She laughed.

"Don't worry about me. I'll be alright. But please do take better care of yourself. How is your wound?"

"It's coming along. My limp is not so pronounced now."

Martin took his mother's hands in his and looked at her for a long time before speaking.

"Mother, I've done some things . . . things I would like to forget, but can't."

"I know, son. War's a terrible business. Bad things happen."

Martin grew quiet for a moment before continuing.

"I was a part of Einsatzgruppe D in the Ukraine. Major Steiner said what we had to do was an unpleasant but necessary task in order to secure living space and protect the Reich. He said it was like our promised land. But I'm not so sure. Some of the things I did . . . I don't think you and Father would approve . . . there were women and children involved."

Her thin, frail hands tightened their grip on his.

"Martin, you are my son. War can make people do bad things. No matter what happened or what you did—none of it will change my feelings for you."

"But Mother, I'm not sure if you knew what I did, you would. . ."

She interrupted him.

"A Mother's love forgives all. Always remember that."

"I'll try Mother."

"Good."

The rain began to fall again.

"Martin, someone is coming."

He turned to the sound of footsteps. Rising, he kissed his her on the cheek.

"It's Major Mueller and the American Captain, and some other officer. I'll see what they want. I'll only be a minute."

Sergeant Luther took his Zippo out of his pocket and lit Captain Ember's cigarette. The rain began to fall harder. Turning up the collar of his overcoat, he watched the two MP's drag the struggling German officer toward their jeep.

His cries pierced the silence. "Mutter. Mutter"

Luther accepted a cigarette from the pack Barris offered him.

"That might just be the damnedest thing I've seen in this war yet. I'll bet that fellow is headed straight to the nut house."

Barris kicked a clump of mud with his boot.

"I'd say that's a pretty safe bet."

"Why you reckon he did that?"

"Did what?"

The Sergeant flicked the ash from his cigarette butt.

"You know, picked that particular body out of a pit full o' dead ones, tied a red scarf around her neck, and came to think she was his Momma. And a Jew at that. What makes a man do that?"

Barris Embers put his hands in his coat pocket.

"Don't really know. Wouldn't be surprised if there's not some buzzards circling close by."

Clearing his throat, he spit into the mud.

"Let's go get some chow."

5

The Last Prayer Meeting

It was more of a winter than a winter ought to be. A cold shroud of snow and ice fell from a dark gray blanket of a hidden sky and seeped deep into the marrow of men in foxholes. It seemed to most that hell had finally frozen over, especially when a German ghost army slithered in through the Ardennes Forest, their 88s raining down fire and brimstone. The clackety-clack of their Tiger and Panther tanks and massive, fast-moving attacks from Panzer and SS units caught the Americans by surprise. What was thought to be a probing sortie, was anything but that. When all seemed lost, the skies opened and the allied planes came.

Rayfield Jackson and the rest of his platoon gathered around Sergeant Altus McFadden "Alright, men, listen up. Those German bastards are in retreat so we will be doing some mop-up after morning chow. We know what they did to our boys at Malmedy. And a couple of weeks back when we captured those Hitler Jugend boy soldiers and told them to go home, they ambushed us two days later. So I want to be clear. I better not see anybody coming back with German POWs. Man or boy, only dead Germans can't shoot."

Bright sunlight bounced off snow laden branches of beech, poplar and pine trees. Rayfield found the crunch of the frozen ground unsettling as he made his way through the forest shadows in search of German stragglers. The sound of a gunshot here and there signaled another German threat snuffed out. Cradling his M1 carbine in the crook of his arm, he pulled a cigarette out of his jacket pocket and lit it. The second draw on his cigarette was interrupted by a cough to his right. Safety off, he lowered his rifle and peered into a stand of black pines. Squinting, he could make out the shape of a man sitting on a rucksack, leaning back against the tree. Kneeling, Rayfield prepared to shoot. A rasping cough, followed by another.

The man turned his head toward the American and called out in perfect English, "I am not armed. I am wounded and would like to surrender."

Rayfield circled to his left until he was satisfied the German soldier was alone and unarmed. Stepping out from behind a large pine, he looked down the barrel of his rifle into the eyes of a wounded adversary.

"You alone?"

The German winced. "Yes, I got separated from my unit and given my wounds, couldn't keep up."

Rayfield peered at the wounded enemy soldier. "How come you speak English?"

"Born and bred in the Queens section of New York City," the German replied with a forlorn smile.

"The hell you say. If that's the case, what you doing in a German uniform?"

The Landser shifted slightly and moaned. "Against my parents' wishes, my older brother returned to Germany to fight for what he believed was the Fatherland—before America was involved. I joined him a year later."

Rayfield leaned in for a closer look. "Looks like your shoulder's busted up and a bad bleed coming from your thigh."

The German nodded. "Shell fragments from one of your mortars. Any chance you might give me a drink of water?"

Rayfield thought for a moment, then handed the wounded German his canteen. Placing his carbine against a tree, he kneeled down and began to fashion a tourniquet to stop the bleeding.

The German screwed the lid back on the canteen. "Thank you. My name's Martin—Martin Messer. May God bless you for your kindness."

Rayfield looked up from the bandage he had fashioned around the wounded soldier's leg. "May God bless you? What kind of NAZI are you? Anyway, I don't see much evidence of God in these parts."

"The Lutheran kind," Martin replied. "My mother was Catholic and my father, a Lutheran. And I get your point about God . . . It feels like that . . . about Him not being around. My older brother convinced me that we would help rebuild the Fatherland. At least, that's what we thought."

"How'd that work out for you?" Rayfield replied, stuffing his first-aid kit into his backpack.

A wave of sorrow washed over the German's face. "Not so good. We didn't want to believe what was happening until it was too late."

Martin groaned as he shifted his weight. "What about you?"

"What about me what?" Rayfield replied, fishing a cigarette out of his jacket pocket.

"I'm guessing you are Presbyterian, Methodist, maybe even Catholic?"

Rayfield lit the cigarette from the one he was smoking and handed it to the wounded German.

"Baptist born and bred. In West Virginia farm country most folks are Baptist."

The two men smoked in silence.

Martin pulled a worn photograph from his tunic. "This is my wife, Julia. And my two daughters, Romy, named after my mother and Lily, the baby."

Rayfield flicked the ash from the end of his cigarette. "Nice looking family."

"How about you?"

The American hesitated before turning back to the German.

"Name's Rayfield. Most folks call me Ray. No kids. Me and Matilda—I call her Tildy, tied the knot before I shipped out. We decided to wait on babies in case I don't . . . anyway, looks like the bleeding's slowed down."

Martin took another drink from Ray's canteen and handed it back to him. "I have been praying a lot lately. I find comfort in the 23rd Psalm a lot lately. 'Though I walk through the valley of the shadow of death . . .'"

"John."

"John?"

"Yeah, John. That verse where it says not to let your heart be troubled. That's my go to verse when I can't sleep and feel . . . Anyway . . ." Ray's voice trailed off.

Martin looked up through the trees and returned his gaze to Ray.

"I would like to say a prayer for you and Tildy."

"Pray for me and my wife?"

"Yes . . . for you and your wife."

Ray rubbed the stubble on his chin and considered the German's request. "Hell, why not?"

When Martin finished, Ray coughed and cleared his throat, and returned the favor, praying for Martin's wife and two daughters."

Ray lit another cigarette. "Guess I've now seen it all. Two enemies praying for each other in the middle of a war. Killing each other one day and praying each other the next. It's enough to make a man's head hurt."

Martin reached out and grasped Ray by the hand. "In God's kingdom, we aren't enemies. We are brothers in Christ."

Rising to his feet, Ray's eyes glistened. "True enough. And I wish we could fly away from this place. But we can't."

Looking down at Martin, he adjusted his helmet's chin strap. "I wish things were different. You might be my brother in Christ, but you aren't my brother in arms."

Ray flipped what was left of his cigarette to the ground and stomped it out with the heel of his boot. "Sarge gave strict orders to take no prisoners and where I come from, no matter how hard, orders are orders."

Ray retrieved his carbine. "I'll see you on the other side."

Martin pressed the photograph of Julia, Romy and Lily to his chest and closed his eyes.

A single shot echoed through the wounded trees of the Ardennes.

6

Dead Man's Parade

"WHEN WE MARCHED DOWN them streets of New York City after the war with all that spit and polish and them bands playing, I swear on my mother's grave, I could see those dead boys we left behind marching with us." Big Tiny nodded his head in agreement, but said nothing as he and Abernathy drank in silence.

A bluebird landed on a tree branch and announced its presence. Abernathy sloshed some more corn liquor into his tin cup. "Wasn't no blue bird songs on the battlefields in France or at the Bulge. Only dying songs sung there. Men screaming for their mommas. I still dream about those boys—white and black."

Big Tiny nodded once more. "Could'a been a thousand of them blue birds and you still couldn't a' heard they song."

The row of Shanties stood in a row as if standing at attention and saluting the ripe cotton fields lying before them as far as the eye could see. Weather worn and unpainted, rust covered tin roofs offered their inhabitants a modest measure of protection against the elements. The black tenant families toiled in the fields of white farmers in a nod to the past when they were considered property. Now they were free, free for the most part to be poor and submissive to the descendants of past Masters—slaves to ghosts of the past.

Big Tiny turned up the jug and wiped his mouth with the back of his hand. "I woke in a sweat night before last dreamin' 'bout them damn Krauts. They 88's done took out our tank and there they was, four of them grinin' and pointin' that big gun right at me."

Abernathy took a can of Prince Albert out of his overall pocket and rolled himself a cigarette. "No need for you to run. As big as you is and as big as that 88 was, ain't no way they gonna miss."

Big Tiny swatted at a fly buzzing near his head. "Like I said, it was a dream. Bad as it was, I still here."

Abernathy took a long draw off his cigarette. "Truth is, they wasn't no grinning Krauts on the day you got hold o' that .50 caliber on the tank's turret. Like the 761st motto says you 'come out fightin'. You might not 'a looked like no black panther, but from where I was, you damn sure looked like a big ol' black bear. They might 'a stopped your tank, but they didn't stop Big Tiny. How come you didn't run for cover like the rest o' us?"

"Don't know for sure," Big Tiny replied with a shrug. "They blew up our tank and killed two good boys, one from New York and the other—I can't remember where he from. Anyways, I was trying to help Henry get off the tank and them bastards shot me in the ass. When my back was turned, they shot me in the ass. How that gonna look—me being shot in the ass?"

Big Tiny turned up the jug once more. "That made me sho' nuff mad. I be so mad I thought I would bust. I guess I more mad than scared. Don't remember much after that. Reckon the Devil got hold o' me."

Rolling another cigarette, Abernathy looked at his friend and grinned. "Only devil present that day, was the devil you gave them Jerrys."

"Reckon you right," Big Tiny replied.

"Damn straight, I'm right. The Colonel hisself came down to shake you hand and pin that Purple Heart on you."

Abernathy flicked a strand of tobacco off his tongue and chuckled. "Whoeee, a black man from Mississippi shoots 12 white men dead, even if they was Germans and gets a handshake and Purple Heart for doing it. Never thought I would see such."

Big Tiny's face clouded over. "They's a couple of white men 'round these parts I'd like to join them Krauts, starting with Billy Thompson."

"He ain't but 14, Big Tiny, more like a 14-year-old beanpole."

The cloud grew darker. "He a beanpole with a mean mouth. Try to boss me 'round like his Daddy do. Cusses me and calls me a n . . . . His Daddy pay my wages. He don't."

Abernathy reached over and squeezed his friend's shoulder. "Little Billy piss-pot don't know no better. He just actin' out what his Daddy thinkin'. I s'pect if he knew what you did to them Krauts, he might be more careful."

His friend's words pushed away the cloud. "I s'pect so. If'n he saw what I did over there, he wouldn't want to rile me."

"Might even wet his beanpole pants," Abernathy replied, holding out his cup for a refill. "You show Tildy and your folks your medal?"

"Yeah, I showed 'em ," Big Tiny nodded. "Daddy told me to hide it and he right to tell me that. Fact is, he told me not to wear my uniform home so when the bus stopped in Virginia, I put on 'share croppin' clothes . . . packed my uniform away. Daddy said Reverend Soloman told him 'bout a boy down in Mobile who wore his Bronze Star pinned on his uniform downtown. Three white men beat him to death on the edge o' town when he was walking home."

Big Tiny bowed his head. "Mmm. Mmm. They beat that poor boy to death right in front o' his wife and chillun'."

Abernathy blew a smoke ring spiraling up into the evening air. "Heard they lynched a black soldier last month in Jackson cause someone saw a picture of a white woman in his wallet. More'n likely one of them Frenchies."

Big Tiny turned and looked at his friend. "Ab, what we fightin' for? Our blood just as red as theirs."

The sun was beginning to set behind the tree line. "The white folk think we fightin' for them, but we—I ain't really. What did you and me see on our leave in Paris?"

"We saw the biggest city I ever saw."

Abernathy continued. "And the people?"

Big Tiny scratched his scruff of a beard. "They was nice. They looked at us different—like we like them. When that ol' white French lady hugged and thanked me, it 'bout scared me to death. Thought maybe a lynch party might be hidin' somewhere 'round the corner."

"You told it right when you said they looked at us like we was the same as them. Me and you didn't have to look down at our feet when folks was talkin' to us and say yes suh and no ma'am. We wasn't n***s in Paris, France. We was men—fightin' men o' the 761st—fightin' for they and our freedom. We was men."

Crickets began to sing in unison as nighttime approached. Big Tiny's wife, Tildy, walked out on the porch and placed her hands on her hips. "You two boys done had enough o' the jug. Time for y'all to come inside and eat your supper while it's hot. I already fed the chillun."

Fried rabbit and okra covered a cracked earthenware platter. Collard greens simmered in a pot on the wood stove and a pone of cornbread cooled in the cast iron skillet. A small plate was stacked high with fresh sliced tomatoes. After Big Tiny said the blessing, the friends began to eat.

"My, my Tildy, ain't no one cook like you," Abernathy said, smacking his lips. "No wonder Big Tiny as big as he is."

Tildy rolled her eyes. "Ab, you one sweet-talkin' fool, but I already married so you might as well save your shuck and jive for some other woman."

The three of them laughed. Big Tiny buttered a piece of cornbread. "Tildy shore nuff got your number, Ab."

When supper was finished, Tildy rose from the table. "You two go back out on the porch. I cook up some chicory coffee and bring you a cup."

The two of them sat on the porch steps. Abernathy rolled another cigarette and Big Tiny packed his corncob pipe with Prince Albert. Abernathy handed his Zippo lighter to Tiny. "You hit the jackpot with Tildy. Hope you know it."

"I reckon I did," Big Tiny smiled. "She a good woman."

After Tildy brought them their coffee, they smoked and sipped from their cups in silence, listening to the sounds of the night.

"In 'bout another week, it be hot in them fields," Big Tiny said relighting his pipe, "No time for restin' in the shade if you want to make a few dollars from old man Thompson. He fair enough compared to some o' the other farmers. Lets us tenant families get vegetables from the big garden, gives us some ham and beef when butchering time comes."

Abernathy pulled a toothpick out of his shirt pocket. "Fair enough ain't none too fair considerin' the fact that you and your family be laboring from dawn 'til dark pickin' cotton and such."

"Got nothin' to do with fair. Got everything to do with puttin' food on the table and a roof over you and you family's head. What 'bout Mr. Robert Lee Higgs. How he treatin' you?"

"He a good man," Abernathy replied. "Don't talk much, but more'n fair for a white man in these parts. You remember when that Klan member, Mr. Jacob Mosely, threatened Moss Higgins with burnin' him and his family out so he could get they land? Well, Mr. Bob told Moss to turn his wagon 'round and go home. He talked to Mosely and that was that."

Big Tiny leaned back on his elbows. "I do remember. First time a white man stand up for us 'round here. Still, why he make you work on Sunday? Even sharecroppers get the Lord's day off."

Abernathy laughed. "He don't make me. He doing me a favor. He know I a better mechanic than Petey Dawson and Homer. Remember how I get those tanks and jeeps up and runnin' when we was overseas?"

"Mmhmm," Big Tiny replied.

"He also know how people 'round here feel about a black man betterin' hisself. So while I step and fetch it during the week, he open up the shop for me on Sunday after church and let me work on trucks and tractors. When he come back by at the end o' the day, he pay me in cash—the same he pay Petey and Homer."

Big Tiny's eye widened. "He do? What Petey and Homer think 'bout that?"

"They think Mr. Bob doing the work hisself," Abernathy chuckled. "Last week, I hear Petey tell Homer he can't believe Mr. Robert Lee Higgs workin' on Sunday."

Both men laughed at the thought of it.

"How them two to work with?"

Abernathy took a sip of coffee. "They no better or worse than other white folk. Homer a lot like Mr. Bob—he don't say much. Petey Dawson a little man with big man desires. He like to tease me about how the Army couldn't teach a n*** how to be a real mechanic. Little do he know."

Dogs barked in the distance.

"Ab, when you ever gonna find a woman and settle down? Ain't right a man of you age not havin' a woman and some chillun."

Abernathy took his time responding to his friend's question. "Remember the dreams we had we was walkin' free in Paris, France. Remember how we breathed easy there?"

"Yeah, I do," Big Tiny replied. "But that dreamin' in the past. Time to put roots down. A wife, chillun' and such. 'Sides dreamin' too much in these parts can get a man in trouble—maybe even killed."

Swallowing the last of his coffee, Abernathy agreed. "Yeah, it can. You dream in the past. You have a wife, chillun' and family 'round here. I don't 'cause I be travelin' light. My dream pullin' me toward the future."

"We be you family," Big Tiny replied, his voice full of emotion.

The two men grew quiet. Abernathy reached over and patted Big Tiny on the leg. "You always be my family. 'Though that always be, I need to breathe easy."

Big Tiny shrugged. "Where you gonna breathe easy 'round here?"

"I ain't," Abnernathy replied. "My dream pullin' me toward Detroit where they makin' all them cars and trucks. A good mechanic could find plenty o' work there and good wages too."

"Ab, Detroit ain't no Paris, France. I s'pect they's plenty o' Petey Dawson's up there."

Abernathy took a draw off of his cigarette. "You probably right 'bout that."

"You boys 'bout ready for bed? Tomorrow's church day," Tildy hollered from inside.

"I be hittin' the road, Tildy. Got to be at Mr. Bob's shop tomorrow," Abernathy replied, rising from the steps.

Tildy walked out onto the porch. "I ain't studyin' you walkin' them roads tonight. Saturday night's ripe with white trash drinkin' and ridin' the roads looking for a black man to gang up on. You stay with us and I fix you some breakfast fore we go to church meetin'."

Big Tiny looked at Abernathy. "Best do what she say when she got that tone."

Abernathy smiled. "Thank you kindly, Tildy. If you got a blanket, I just sleep out here on the porch where it cool. No need for breakfast. I ate so much supper, I won't be hungry. I be leavin' early."

"Suit yourself," Tildy laughed. "Ain't no such thing as cool in these parts."

Abernathy walked along the road toward town, singing to himself. A new day was dawning. The sky was blue—not a cloud in sight. He hummed "Deep River" and thought to himself, "I don't know 'bout crossin' over into Jordan, but I sho' enough wouldn't mind crossin' over into Detroit." He smiled. "I wonder how long it take a man to walk there."

7

Virgil's Solace

THE EIGHTEEN-WHEELER BELLOWED AND belched its way down Highway 33 through the cracked, black two-lane yellow pine forests. Six miles this side of "Joe Wheeler's Barbecue Palace", Eugene McReady did what he had done three times a week for the last seven years. He looked to his left at the small unpainted clapboard farmhouse perched on what passed for a hill in southwest Tennessee and pulled his horn for three short bursts.

Virgil Murdock sat where he always did—third step from the bottom that led to the covered porch of the house he shared with Amos and Margie-Lee Murdock, his father and mother. To the occasional visitor, Virgil seemed to sit "at attention," as though he was waiting for some hidden command or marching orders. His posture wasn't one of relaxed repose or whimsical self-reflection. Rigid and stoic, Virgil looked as though he were leaning into his silence in anticipation of something unseen but still felt—some faint dread or unwelcome visitation. His gaze remained steady throughout the day, placed just above the tree-line's horizon on the other side of highway 33, the only exception was occasional furtive glances toward the creek and woods down the hill to his right. Those brief interruptions looked to his parents like momentary distractions from his primary meditation, sometimes accompanied by the slightest hint of pleasantness; on other occasions followed by a fearful stare.

Sitting at attention on his step of preference, Virgil waited patiently for three events around which his solitary existence revolved—his father's return from work at the sawmill, his mother calling him for lunch or supper, and Eugene McReady's greeting and acknowledgment which arrived three times a week.

The horn's three short blasts turned Virgil's head. His eyes and the corners of his mouth crinkled into the closest thing to a smile anyone in Elbert County would see from Virgil, except when his father rubbed his back each evening after supper.

There had been a brief period of time three years ago when Amos and Margie-Lee's spirits had soared at the possibility of a miracle.

Their hope began when Eugene McReady parked his eighteen-wheeler on the shoulder of the road just past Murphy's General Store around lunch time in order to purchase a Coca Cola and a bologna and cheese sandwich. While waiting to order, he overheard the store's owner, Red Murphy, and two elderly patrons talking about Virgil's state of mind.

"I tell you, the boy ain't been right since the war," Red exclaimed as he poked a fresh-cut wedge of Red Man chewing tobacco into his mouth.

"I ain't so sure 'bout that, Red. As I think back, Virgil was always a little strange. Even when he was a boy, I can remember some peculiarities like the time . . ."

"Shut your mouth, Peety Matthews," shouted a large bald-headed man in worn denim overalls, pointing his finger at the smaller man. "You callin' anybody peculiar is like the pot calling the kettle black. Besides, Virgil's a veteran. He served his country for the likes of you and me and paid one hell of a price! He's up there sitting on those steps reliving all that terror while me and you are down here with Red, sipping colas and eatin' candy bars. You ought to be ashamed of yourself."

Peety's face turned crimson. "I didn't mean no disrespect. I was just speaking my mind."

J.D. ground out the butt of his hand-rolled cigarette in the ashtray on the counter.

"No disrespect, my ass," he scoffed. "If you spoke your mind like that on Wednesday evenings when Amos comes by for his weekly game of checkers with Red, he'd throw your scrawny ass out in the street."

"Now boys, settle down," Red chimed in, spitting a stream of tobacco juice into an empty Maxwell House coffee can on the floor. "We've got a customer here who needs waitin' on."

The two old-timers looked at the newcomer and returned to their seats around the warmth of the potbellied stove. For a time, the only sounds were the popping of the stove's hot sheet metal as Eugene ate his lunch.

Finally, Red broke the silence.

"I noticed you been stoppin' from time to time. Where you haulin' all that produce?"

Pausing between mouthfuls of bologna and cheese, Eugene took a long drink of Coca Cola before responding.

"Got me a new route. Three times a week to the train depot at Higgsville. From there I reckon they ship the produce to Memphis and beyond."

Eugene finished the last of his cold drink and placed the empty bottle on the counter.

"Sorry to hear about the fellow who's having trouble."

Red's eyes narrowed slightly. "Yeah, it's a shame."

"Yeah, it is. There's a lot of folks who came back like . . ."

"His name's Virgil," Red interjected.

"Truth is, I was a lot like Virgil the first year I got back. Couldn't sleep. Drank too much. Nightmares. Stuff like that."

J.D and Peety roused out of their collective sulking and perked up. Clearing his throat, Red relaxed a bit and looked squarely at Eugene.

"Where did you serve?"

Lost in a moment's reflection, Eugene replied softly, "Infantry . . . two years in Europe. Where did Virgil serve?"

J.D rose to his feet and approached Eugene, followed by a subdued Peety.

"Virgil served in Europe too. Fought in the Battle of the Bulge. Krauts overran his unit. Him and one other fella were the only ones who survived."

"That was one hell of a fight. Lot of good men died. But then, a lot of good men always die in war."

J.D. extended his hand to Eugene. "Were you at the Bulge?"

Eugene took J.D.'s hand. "Yeah, I was at Bastogne."

J.D. became more animated. "Did you know Virgil? Matter o' fact, I lost a cousin in that battle. Name of Eli Givins. You ever hear of him?"

"Don't believe I knew Virgil or Eli. Things were crazy. The whole time was kind of a blur. Don't remember a lot of details. Some that I do remember, I wish I didn't."

Red sighed. "After Virgil recovered from his wounds, they assigned him to the burial detail. All them poor boys—their bodies stacked like cordwood—it was too much for Virgil. He went downhill from there. They ended shipping him to a Veteran's hospital down in Louisiana. He wasn't right in his mind. Amos couldn't get off work at the sawmill so his poor Mama had to go all the way to Louisiana and fetch him herself."

A thin bead of sweat broke out on Eugene's forehead.

Bodies . . . stacked . . . cordwood. Eugene felt a rush of the past blow by him. The room seemed uncomfortably warm. He looked at his watch, then at the three older men. "Fellas, it's been nice meeting you. I got to get on down to Higgsville with my load. Be sure to give Virgil and his family my best."

Red and Peety spoke in unison, "Same to you . . ."

"Name's Eugene."

As he turned to leave, Red tossed a Hershey bar to him.

"It's on the house."

That's how it started—how Amos and Margie-Lee began to hope in the possibility that their son might one day return from no-man's-land. And for the first month or two, their dreams of rescue like the promise of the coming spring, held them breathless.

From their first meeting, the two men hit it off. Perhaps, it was a tilt of the head or a hint of the haunted memories that combat veterans share. Whatever it was, Eugene and Virgil quickly progressed from "how do you do's" to more private conversations sitting on the front steps of Murphy's store while Red and Virgil's father played checkers inside under the watchful eyes of Peety and J.D. The four men marveled at how Eugene McReady drew Virgil out. Checkers became an excuse for them to gather and listen in reverence for the rustle of salvation in the evening breeze. Eugene, the shepherd, guiding Virgil, the wounded, lost sheep back to the fold. They strained to listen for the sounds of Virgil's return from theland of the lost and the dead. The four men's whispers were like children's prayers, calling for the magical return of their beloved. The high point of their Wednesday evening vigil was the night they heard Virgil laugh for the first time since he returned from the war. He was like the Virgil of old, laughing spontaneously from deep within his belly. The four men held their breath, rapt in wonder and awe at the sound of such a thing.

And then, as quickly as Virgil had stepped forward into the light, he retreated back into the shadows of his past.

Red poured a cup of coffee and handed it to Eugene.

"I still can't believe Virgil quit showing up on Wednesdays. Seemed like he was coming out of his slump. 'Specially after we heard him laugh that one night. That was sure enough a sound for sore ears."

Eugene sipped the hot coffee.

"Yeah, I know what you mean. Coming back from the likes of what Virgil saw can be a tricky business. Had a fella in my platoon from Texas by the name of Roman Gidensky. We all called him Romeo. He got hit by a piece of shrapnel from a German 88 and was carted off to the field hospital. He seemed fine when he returned, joking with everybody and showing off his Purple Heart. One morning out of the blue, Romeo just shut down. Nobody knew why. He wouldn't talk to anybody, even the company commander. He just sat looking at his purple heart, smoking one cigarette after another."

Red reached for the coffee pot.

"What happened to your friend?"

Eugene stuck his cup out for a refill.

"Don't know. Never heard from him again."

The two men drank their coffee in silence and listened to the sound of a tractor turning the soil for spring planting in a nearby field.

Virgil's retreat found Amos and Margie-Lee slipping back into their routine as before only sadder. Virgil spent most of his day sitting at attention, third step from the bottom, watching for the ghosts in the woods. He listened patiently for Margie-Lee's mealtime commands and Eugene's thrice weekly horn-blowing salutes. More than anything else though, Virgil listened for the sound of his Daddy's footsteps creaking their way across the weathered front porch after supper and the tender touch that followed.

Amos rubbed his son's back and shoulders with strong hands, carefully kneading and loosening the knots of tension and fear. Virgil would occasionally exhale a low moan as his body relaxed from the pressure of his father's practiced fingers. During the countless hours Amos massaged his son's back and shoulders, he found himself imagining that his hands held magical powers—that he could apply that same, strong delicate touch to Virgil's broken mind and spirit.

"Did you hear from Eugene today?" Amos said. "He's letting his boy, Eddie, ride with him when he makes his run to Higgsville."

"Yessir. Three blows of the horn, same as usual."

Amos stopped momentarily to fish tobacco out of his sweat-stained khakis and rolled himself a cigarette. "That Eugene's a fine fellow."

Amos lit his cigarette and resumed rubbing Virgil's back while Virgil looked toward the highway and down at the woods.

"You know, Daddy, Eugene's the only person who knows what I went through—what went through me."

Amos flicked the ash from the end of his cigarette and coughed.

Virgil continued when he felt his father's hands return.

"I knew Eugene understood the first night you introduced me to him at Murphy's store. It was in his eyes. A man can't hide that look. He'd like to, but he can't." Virgil's voice trailed off.

Amos patted his son's head, signaling the end of the evening's back-rub.

"Honeysuckle smells good."

It had been a good evening. Father and son together, enjoying a warm summer night, listening to the serenade of crickets and Margie-Lee, wife of one and Mother to the other, humming "Amazing Grace" while she cleaned up the kitchen.

The following week, Amos was diagnosed with lung cancer.

Six months to the day after Doc Brown's diagnosis, Amos died.

The day before Amos's funeral, Virgil killed himself.

"I surely do miss Amos," J.D. lamented as he sat on a coca cola crate, leaning against the wall of Murphy's storefront.

"That was one sad sight," Peety groaned in agreement. "Father and son, buried at the same time, side by side. Why in the world would Virgil put the barrel of his Daddy's shotgun in his mouth and pull the trigger in the middle of highway 33?"

Red wiped the summer heat dripping from his brow with the back of his hand.

"Don't have no idea. Poor Margie-Lee. 'Course, she couldn't have managed Virgil by herself. Maybe it was a blessing of sorts."

J.D. stretched his legs out in front of him.

"Maybe so. Or maybe he thought that was the only way he could go a'lookin' for his Daddy. Reverend Hamm says Margie-Lee plans to sell the home place and move in with her widowed sister in Tuscaloosa."

Red popped a piece of gum in his mouth.

"It's probably for the best."

The eighteen-wheeler leaned into a familiar curve on highway 33 with a roar. Loaded with corn bound for the depot at Higgsville, Eugene watched his son fiddle with the radio.

Eddie looked up at his father and smiled. "Daddy, can I blow the horn for Virgil?"

Turning to his son, he gently squeezed his shoulder.

"Yes, Eddie, blow the horn for Virgil."

8

Safe Landing

THE HARVEST THAT GREW in the loamy soil in the county of Suffolk would have to wait after the Americans arrived. Crushed stones from broken pieces of London transformed wheat fields and vegetable gardens into runways where instruments of survival and retribution descended in droves. In short order, farm fields became air fields, home to B-17 Flying Fortresses and B-24 Liberators complements of the United States Eighth Air Force.

The big birds took off with a roar for their daylight bombing runs, sometimes as few as a dozen or so and on other missions several hundred took flight. Young boys and old men watched for their return. Always fewer in number, some relatively intact and others trailing smoke from the sky, flying on a wing and a prayer. If pilots or crew members survived 25 bombing runs, they were relieved from flying duty. Some did. Many didn't. The average life expectancy of a crewman in 1943 was eleven missions.

Captain Edward Hampshire, the RAF liaison officer, drummed his fingers on the table in the empty officer's mess while his American counterpart, Captain Wes Baker looked over the daily report.

He smiled at his fellow officer. "How about a cuppa of good English tea?"

"You know damn well, I prefer my coffee black, hot with nothing added," Wes Baker replied without looking up.

Alone in the lounge, the two men sipped their tea and coffee.

Wes Baker stared at the window. It was beginning to rain.

"That rain isn't going to help the crews returning from their sortie."

Ed tamped tobacco into his pipe and lit it. "The boys have been through a lot—we all have. Especially with the daylight raids in '43 before we got fighter escorts."

Wes took a sip of coffee. "Bremen, Regensburg, Halberstadt and the ball bearing plant in Shweinfurt. I don't know how any of us made it back from Shweinfurt."

"Black Thursday," Ed replied, relighting his pipe. "They limped back, three with engines on fire, not to mention wounded, dead and missing crewmen. There must have been two hundred or more German fighters harassing the B-17s all the way."

Wes looked at his hands. "Out of almost 300 bombers, only 33 made it back undamaged."

Both men grew silent, lost in the weight of it all.

Ed Hampshire got up from the table and returned with fresh cups of hot tea and coffee.

"Wes, do you mind me asking you a question?"

Wes drank from the steaming cup. "Ask Away, Captain."

"I noticed every time you return from a mission, the first thing you do is walk down to that stand of beech and maple trees and stay for quite a while. You are the only one that does that and I was just wondering why?"

Wes rubbed his eyes and looked back out at the rain. "I do two things. I thank God for sparing my life and keeping my crew safe. I thank God for giving us life and breath for one more day."

Wes returned to his coffee.

"And the other thing?"

Looking up from his coffee, Wes seemed to stare into a distance only he could see.

"I ask God to forgive me for all the people killed when we dropped those bombs."

9

Hold the Line

THE SWELTERING HEAT SEEMED to suck the oxygen out of the small, dilapidated shack where the two GIs were holed up. Ray lit another cigarette off Morgan's. "You see any movement out there?"

Morgan took off his helmet and wiped sweat from his brow. "Not since we took care of that recon patrol this morning. 'Course, who knows when they'll send another one? How's our ammo holding out?"

"We're down to two grenades," Ray replied. "We're ok with the machine guns."

Morgan peered through the binoculars at the hedgerow and tree line. "Whatever it takes, we've got to hold the line."

He tossed his cigarette butt on the floor of the shack and ground it out with his boot. "These Winston's are ok, but I like the taste of the Menthols better."

Ray blew a smoke ring. "Yeah, me too. What kind of rations we got left?"

Rummaging through his field pack, Morgan handed Ray a canteen. "Looks pretty good. Two canteens full of grape Kool-Aid, one pimento cheese sandwich, one peanut butter and jelly and four graham crackers. We ate the sardines yesterday. You want peanut butter and jelly or pimento cheese?"

Ray flipped the remains of his cigarette out of the window as he quickly scanned the tree line for any sign of enemy activity. "How about pimento cheese? I had peanut butter and jelly for supper last night."

Morgan handed his friend a sandwich. "One pimento cheese coming up."

The field rations menu for sixth grade warriors was limited. The two boys washed down their rations with grape Kool-Aid.

Ray stretched and yawned. "I tried to snatch some menthols from my mother's stash, but she was out so I had sneak a pack from my Dad's carton of Winston's."

Tapping a cigarette against the pack like they do in the movies, Morgan wedged it behind his ear and looked out the window. "Sometimes you have to make do with what you can get. By the way, my mom's coming to pick me up around five o'clock."

"Five!" Ray exclaimed. "I thought you'd be spending the night. Don't you remember the plan for our nighttime raid? I even got face paint."

Morgan took the cigarette from behind his ear and lit it. "I know, I know. Trouble is, my mom outranks me. I'll be tied up every evening this week."

"Doing what?" Ray queried fishing another Winston out of the pack.

"Vacation Bible School."

Ray fumbled with the matches. "All week?"

"Yep," Morgan replied. "All week."

Slinging his helmet to the floor, Ray shrugged in exasperation. "Well, hell, it is what it is. I guess we'll have to postpone night maneuvers until next week."

"Guess so," Morgan said as he drained the last of the Kool-Aid from his canteen and smacked his lips.

Ray kicked his field pack. "Wait a minute! Next week my dad has to go for his appointment at the Veteran's hospital."

Morgan perked up. "You never told me your Daddy was a veteran. What was he—army, navy, marines?"

"Air Force. He was a fighter pilot in Europe. Flew a P-51 Mustang," Ray replied softly.

"Fighter pilot! Hot damn, a fighter pilot. I can't believe you never told me he was a fighter pilot. And he flew a P-51 Mustang—king of the skies!"

Morgan looked like he was ready to dance a jig. "I just finished reading a library book about German fighter pilots. I bet your Daddy has some tales to tell. How many Messerschmitt 109s and Fock-Wulfes did he shoot down?"

"I don't know."

"You don't know?" Morgan continued. "I can't believe you don't know that. Well, we'll just have to ask him."

Ray looked at his hands. "We can't."

Morgan looked at his friend incredulously. "Why the hell not?"

"Because I'm not supposed to know," Ray replied quietly. "Since you're my best friend, I'll tell you why as long as you promise not to tell anyone else."

Ray grabbed Morgan's wrist and looked at him with all the solemnity a boy his age could muster. "It's a promise that can't be broken."

Nodding his head to the affirmative, Morgan and Ray sat on their backpacks and lit two fresh cigarettes.

Finally, Ray spoke. "My Mom told me about it so I could understand why my dad acts the way he does. I'm glad she told me because before she did, it could get pretty scary. Two or three times a week my dad wakes up in the middle of the night. Sometimes I can hear him hollering—one time I heard him scream like some wild animal. Then things quiet down. Once I sneaked down the hall and I could hear him crying and my mom whispering to him like she does to me when I have a nightmare. When he wakes up like that, he doesn't go back to sleep. I can hear him walking back and forth on our back porch until the sun comes up. Sometimes, when things get really bad, he goes to the Veterans hospital for a couple of weeks."

Ray paused and turned his head for a moment. "Just a minute, I got something in my eye."

Morgan handed him the pack of Winston's.

Waving off the cigarettes, Ray looked at his friend somberly. "My Dad's squadron fire-bombed Dresden. When he dropped napalm from his plane, he saw women and children running down the street on fire. My Mom said he's never been the same since. The time he woke up screaming, I was worried and tiptoed to their bedroom to see if everything was all right. I stood outside the door and heard my Dad tell my Mom he wished he had died in that fire."

The two friends embraced the silence Ray's testimony demanded.

Ray picked up his army surplus helmet and brushed some dried mud off of it. "My Dad doesn't even want me to play army. Says he heard about plenty of German boy soldiers no older than me who were killed in the fighting."

Morgan reached over and gently patted his friend on the back. "War can sure be a bitch."

"I guess so," Ray muttered as he stared at the floor.

A car horn sounded like a trumpet, displacing the melancholy the two boys shared. Morgan heard his mother calling for him.

Picking up his gear, he turned to Ray. "Maybe we both need a little R and R."

Ray smiled at Morgan. "Vacation Bible School doesn't sound much like R and R to me."

"Better me than you," Morgan hollered as he ran toward his mother's station wagon. "Rest up. Week after next, we'll plan a major offensive."

10

I'll Be Seeing You

WHITE CURTAINS BILLOWED IN a warm summer breeze—blue sky and blue eyes—that's the first thing Jake remembered when he regained consciousness.

The nametag of the nurse checking his blood pressure read "Mildred Scott."

"You've got pretty eyes, Millie."

The young nurse drew back and arched her eyebrow. "Mr. Starnes, you have decided to return to us. Good morning to you."

"Name's Jake. Nice to meet you—"

"Mildred—my name's Mildred," the blue-eyed nurse replied.

Even though his face hurt, Jake smiled anyway. "You're no Mildred. You are definitely a Millie."

Writing down his blood pressure on the medical chart, Mildred looked at the wounded GI who had suddenly become conscious with an amused look. "Is that so, Mr. Jake Starnes?"

"Yep," the young GI replied.

The nurse busied herself checking Jake's wounds.

"You want to know why?" Jake persisted.

"Why what?" she replied as she began dressing the wound on his left arm.

"Why you're a Millie and not a Mildred."

Jake groaned in spite of himself when she pulled the bandage off his rib cage. "Why on earth would I be a Millie rather than the Mildred that I am?"

Jake's throat was dry. He took a sip of water from the cup on his bed-side table. "It's in your eyes. They've got a sparkle to them. Nope, Mildred's too prim and proper a name for you. You are definitely a Millie."

Mildred Scott stared at the GI in bed number 6. "Mr. Starnes, I can't decide whether you are still not fully conscious or if this is the real you?"

Jake cracked another painful grin as he extended the fingers of his right-hand protruding from the cast. "Jake Starnes in the flesh. Pleased to meet you, Millie."

The sea of faces and bandaged bodies that inhabited the convalescent ward painted a picture that only a catastrophe like war could produce. In a sense, the hospital was an oasis—even if temporary—in the midst of war's carnage. The sights and sounds reflected every bit of the fragility of the human condition. Some of the wounded smoked and joked with each other while others chose silence, staring vacantly at nothing in particular. The moans and occasional screams of the more severely wounded provided an absurd contrast to the light banter and bravado of their more am-bulatory comrades. This brotherhood of the wounded came from all walks of life, and every man there, whether he spoke it or not, secretly hoped his wounds would win him a lottery ticket home.

Jake rubbed his fingers across the contours of the belt buckle he held in his good hand. After they killed him, the fellows from his platoon had sent him the sniper's belt buckle as a kind of trophy along with a note. The note said they were surprised how young the German sniper was—that Hitler must be on his last leg if he was sending boys to fight. Of course, Jake knew as well as they did, that boys from the Hitler Jugend were often more fanati-cal and dangerous than regular Wehrmacht soldiers. Jake put the belt buckle and note back in the box. Anyway, a bullet didn't care who pulled the trigger. Still, it sounded like the sniper was about the same age as Bud, Jake's youngest brother back home. Jake lay back on his pillow and thought about the guys in his platoon. He wondered what they were doing.

Jake Starnes and the boys of the 30th Infantry Division didn't go in with the 1st, 29th and 4th Infantry on D-Day. They received their baptism of fire when they relieved the 501st Parachute Regiment and the 101st Airborne on the 15th of June. The battle for St. Lo got serious the first part of July. He could feel the hair on his neck stand up as he recalled fighting in the hedgerows. It was almost like fighting blind. The hedgerows were thick and massive, the Americans on one side and the Germans on the other. One ambush after another, machine gun and rifle fire, grenades, and even hand-to-hand combat were the order of the day. Both sides strained to hear what was happening on the other side of the hedgerows. The snap of a twig, the clanging of a mess kit or the squawk of a radio, could unleash a torrent of fire and a fierce attack. Sometimes sounds were misinterpreted and mistakes were made. Sometimes you shot your own. When that happened, bad dreams were certain to follow.

"Time for lunch, Sergeant Jake Starnes."

That simple announcement—"time for lunch"—pushed the fog of his memories back into the shadows. He looked up. The blue-eyed nurse was back.

"Would you like to try for a short walk outside this afternoon?"

Jake poked his fork at the mashed potatoes. "Depends on who I'm walking with."

The young nurse smiled. "I suppose I could assist you, if you promise to behave."

"It's a date," Jake replied with a thumbs up.

It was warm outside. With Millie's help, Jake slowly made his way along a gravel walking path. A small, well-tended flower garden reminded Jake that something still bloomed besides war.

The two of them found a weatherworn bench outside the canteen entrance. Millie went for coffee and donuts, leaving Jake to rest up from the walk. The sounds of Glenn Miller and Bing Crosby echoed from inside the canteen.

Jake watched Millie sip her coffee and nibble at her donut. "What's it like?"

"What is what like?" Millie replied, brushing crumbs from her lap.

"You know—being a nurse."

Millie didn't know why, but although she was naturally shy regarding personal matters, she found Jake's direct, yet friendly manner, disarming. "The hours are long. There are the blackouts. And of course, there are the patients."

Millie took another sip of coffee. "I remember one 24-hour period when I was responsible for nearly 200 wounded patients spread out in buildings over a city block. There was one poor fellow—he was in terrible shape . . ."

"Worse than me?" Jake interrupted.

A wave of sadness washed over Millie's face. "Yes, much worse than you," she whispered. "As a result of his wounds, he was paralyzed from the neck down."

Jake reached over and gently squeezed Millie's hand.

Millie looked at the turning blades of the ceiling fan on the porch near where they were sitting. "Maybe the most remarkable thing I have observed since being here is how many times a wounded soldier would point out another patient to me, and say "Take care of him first. He's in worse shape than me.""

The two of them sat on the bench listening to the music from the radio inside the canteen.

Bing Crosby crooned "I'll be seeing you in all the old, familiar places."

Jake turned to Millie and said matter-of-factly, "That's our song."

"You don't say," Millie replied, looking at her watch.

"Yep, I do say," Jake responded with a chuckle.

Millie rose from the bench. "Well, Mr. Jake Starnes, what I say is that our pleasant diversion is over. It's time for my rounds."

"Our date."

Millie looked at her watch again and bent over to help Jake stand on his crutches. "Our what?"

As he rose to his feet, Jake's cheek brushed against hers as he whispered in her ear, "Our pleasant 'date' is over."

Night came upon most of the men in the ward with a fitful sleep, or what passed for it, as memories returned to nest in restless minds of the wounded.

The 30th Infantry was ordered to breach the German's defensive line in "Operation Cobra." Re-supplied and bolstered by new replacements, Jake and his platoon mates waited. The Air Corps bombardment would be followed by 50 battalions of artillery pounding the German positions. When H-Hour came, the 30th would move quickly through the hedgerows and penetrate the primary line of German resistance, creating enough room for General Patton's Third Army to pass through, and move quickly toward the Brest Peninsula.

Fifteen minutes before H-Hour, red smoke shells were launched to provide a clear target line for the allied bombers. Problem was, a southern breeze blew the smoke away from the German line toward the 30th Infantry waiting to attack. The result was all hell broke loose. 1500 heavy bombers released their bombs on top of the boys of the 30th Infantry. Almost 200 men were killed or wounded. Since they were held in reserve, Jake's regiment was spared the carnage.

The next day, the same hellish nightmare happened all over again. A southerly breeze pushed the drifting red smoke back on top of the 30th. This time, over 400 men were killed, wounded, or missing in action, including a General and Jake Starnes. When the bombing run had passed, Jake attempted to go to the aid of one of his wounded platoon mates. A sniper's bullet tore through his shoulder, dropping him to the ground. The pain from the shrapnel in his right rib-cage and leg, and his shattered shoulder, reminded him that at least for the moment, he was still alive. Jake remembered thinking just before he lost consciousness that if he didn't have bad luck, he wouldn't have any luck at all.

Bathed in sweat, Jake opened his eyes, expecting to see the dead and dying. Instead, he heard the sound of summer rain and the muted murmur of voices in the ward. He looked at his watch—3 p.m. Tonight, he would meet her at the canteen for lemonade and ice cream. Tomorrow, he would board a Red Cross ship bound for the states where he would have more surgery on his injured leg.

Jake closed his eyes and thought about the last eight weeks. The ghosts of battle often haunted him at night, but in the morning, Millie came and chased those desperate moments away. In the morning, blue-eyed hope appeared announcing the day's possibilities. Jake wondered how could he sail away from what he had found?

Millie and Jake sat on their favorite bench outside the Canteen sipping lemonade on the warm, summer night. The sounds of a local trio played their version of the music of the day—"We'll Meet Again," "Moonlight Serenade," "That Old Black Magic" and "Chattanooga Choo Choo." After a short break, the musicians began playing "I'll Be Seeing You."

Jake turned to Millie. "They're playing our song. Let's dance."

Millie took two quick sips of her lemonade and laughed. "Jake Starnes, have you forgotten that you are still on crutches and your right arm is in a cast?"

Jake struggled to his feet and reaching out his left hand, looked at Millie in a way she hadn't seen before. "It's our song, it's my last night before being shipped back to the states, and it's time to dance."

Taking his hand, Millie kissed him on cheek and put her arms around him. The two of them swayed to the music where they stood, Jake leaning on his crutch and Millie, and she resting her head on his chest. When the music stopped, they continued to sway.

"These have been the best eight weeks of my life," Jake whispered in her ear.

Millie snuggled closer to him.

Jake stopped and tilted Millie's chin with his good hand. "Mildred Scott, I aim to come back after this war's over and marry you."

Millie kissed Jake lightly on the lips. "I hope your aim's good because I will be waiting."

Wartime romances born in the heat of uncertainty had a rhythm all their own. Lovers experienced an intensity of the senses that was often absent in times of peace. The deliberate pace of courtship was swept aside in the tidal pull of living in the moment, when the moment was all you had. Some wartime romances survived and flourished, but most, like Jake and Millie's were lost to distance, duties and plans for a secure future. That didn't mean the sentiments disappeared or were forgotten. Rather, they were locked away in a small, private chamber of the heart, a place where one could visit from time to time and remember.

Jake married Nancy and Millie married James. Jake and Nancy settled in western North Carolina, and raised three daughters while Millie and James ended up in Oklahoma with a son and a daughter. After Nancy died of cancer, Jake puttered around his shop with his best friend, "Mercy", a black lab. He bought a new pick-up truck to celebrate his 80th birthday.

Mildred, who decided after the war that she preferred to be called Millie, received a call from James, Jr. that her husband had died of a massive heart attack while fishing in his beloved bass boat with his son. As he requested, Millie had him buried in his boat with his favorite fishing gear. It took six months for Millie to finish with all the details of living and dying that her life with James represented. Between visits with her daughter Edna and son, James, Jr., and her grandchildren, she began to take an inventory of her life. Old memories and friendships, feelings of gratitude and regret, found their way back into her consciousness.

On a lazy Sunday afternoon, Edna noticed an old photograph album with a bookmark on her mother's bedside table next to the family Bible. Opening the album revealed a picture from another time—a photograph of a smiling young nurse and a GI sitting on a bench holding hands. Edna also discovered a packet of letters in the inside back pocket of the album. Over the next several visits when her mother was working in her vegetable garden, Edna would read one or two of the letters. Finishing the last one, she looked out the window at her mother pruning a rose bush and sighed. Placing the album back in its spot on the table, Edna smiled and waved to her mother.

Jake could see the back of her head. He knew it was her when she took a sip of lemonade—two sips—always two sips—no more, no less. He smiled at Edna and his youngest daughter, Mildred.

The banner across the band's stage read "Senior Center Valentine's Dance." The DJ punched a button and the first strains of "I'll Be Seeing You" began to play. Jake could see her hand holding the lemonade tremble slightly with the song's first notes.

Jake straightened his tie. He never liked them, but tonight he would make an exception. Edna and Mildred watched him limp over to where Millie sat. Bending over, Jake whispered in her ear, "Mildred Scott, may I have this dance?"

Catching her breath, Millie looked at the man standing before her and arched her eyebrow. "Jake Starnes!"

Taking her hand in his, Jake led her to the dance floor. Millie looked at him, her eyes bright with surprise. She kissed him and smiled. "You dancing has improved."

Jake grinned. "I've had 60 years to practice."

Millie kissed him again and nuzzled her head against his chest. The Glenn Miller Orchestra played as Jake and Millie danced into the past.

11

Fire Storm

PETER GLANCED AT A small group of old men clearing rubble from a side street as he straightened his tunic. He looked at the crumpled scrap of paper he held in his hand as though it might magically transport him back to the way things were three years ago. 113 Strasberg Place or what was left of it resonated with the sound of his knuckles rapping against the heavy timbers of the door. Quick, feminine footsteps echoed down the hall. The ancient door slowly creaked open to reveal the face of Anna, the girl he had left behind when he went to fight Russians in the East.

The first look that held Peter and Anna in silent reunion bore witness to the changes in each. In her, the hint of former girlish mischief turned toward a subtle, desperate sorrow and in him, youth's eager ambition replaced by the wary sideways glance of one who had seen things that were best left unseen.

"Peter."

"Anna."

The two joined slowly in an embrace more of relief than passion. Perhaps, those juices might be rekindled, but for now, they clung to the memory of each other. What had been lost was at least for the moment, found.

An older woman bustled through the hallway. "Peter, is that you? Are my eyes playing tricks on me?"

Peter raised his head. "No Frau Rader, I have come for a visit."

Frau Rader's eyes welled up as she took Peter's hands in hers. "We were heartbroken when we heard about your parents—the whole block gone. Such a tragedy."

"Father Thomas said a special prayer at Mass," Anna added.

Peter swatted at a fly. "Wedel is a small town, but still close enough to catch an off-target bombing run."

"You must have been so distressed when you got the news," Frau Rader continued.

Peter reached into his pocket and pulled out a cigarette. "I seem to have gotten used to distress. War is a distressing business that touches everyone in one way or another."

Anna's mother squeezed Peter's hands. "Still, we must celebrate your return. Anna brought a nice sausage home from Herr Bittman's butcher shop this morning. Mr. Bittman has been so good to us during these hard times. I will cook the sausage with some carrots and potatoes I found in the garden."

Peter pulled a package from his knapsack. "I have ersatz coffee, a bit of salt and sugar, and a wedge of cheese." Handing the food to Frau Rader, he remembered a bottle of Schnapps he had been given when he went on leave.

He had not enjoyed a hot meal in weeks. Spearing a piece of potato with his fork, he had forgotten what an excellent cook Frau Rader was. He wondered what Werner, Theo and Erich were eating. Probably soybean sausages and black bread . . . no match for the meal he, Anna and her mother were enjoying. Maybe he could scrounge some real sausages or salt pork to take back to them. He made a mental note not to forget.

After the evening meal, Anna poured coffee for her mother and Peter in the sitting room.

Peter stretched his legs out. "How are the two of you doing?"

Frau Rader smiled, "We are doing well considering the circumstances. As I am sure you noticed, there has been damage from bombing raids, mostly at night."

Anna sipped her coffee and placed her hand on Peter's thigh. "It's mostly the British, but the Americans have also come during the day. At least in the daytime, we are awake and can move more quickly to the shelters. Night-time is the worst."

Frau Rader placed her cup on the small coffee table. "How about you, Peter? We pray for you and our other brave soldiers each day. We ask God for victory and an end to this war. I overheard, Herr Eck, our mayor, at the market the other day say that the Fuhrer is about to unveil a secret weapon that will turn the tide. He was talking to a Wehrmacht officer who assured him that once the Russians were defeated, the British and Americans would be willing to make peace."

Peter shrugged. "I have heard similar reports, but can't say one way or another. If there are such weapons, it would be good to see them put into action. We do the best we can, but there seems to be a lot more of them than us."

Anna's mother poured Peter and herself some Schnapps and began to catch him up with the latest neighborhood gossip. The Schnapps felt good going down. It both warmed and relaxed him. He wondered what Erich, Werner, and Theo were drinking. They had given him the bottle of Schnapps as a present to enjoy on his leave. He hoped they were safe. Frau Rader helped herself to more Schnapps and continued her monologue while Anna snuggled beside him on the couch, gently massaging his neck. Peter's mind drifted to Franz. He would visit Father Thomas tomorrow as Franz had requested. It was a promise he had made that would be kept.

Franz had been a part of their inner circle. He had been a seminary student before the war, a kind of misfit from a military family. In the end, family honor had trumped religious calling. It always seemed odd to the rest of them how at the end of each day, Franz would go off by himself with his New Testament. It was kill or be killed during the day, but when the fighting was over, it was Bible study and prayer time at night, an odd combination to Peter and the others. Time and circumstance finally caught up with his friend. Now he was dead.

Anna's mother rose from her chair. "Peter, the bottle is empty. I have a little apple brandy in the cupboard. Would you like some?"

Her voice brought Peter back to the moment. "Yes, Frau Rader. That would be nice."

Anna smiled and kissed Peter lightly on the cheek. She knew he wasn't paying attention to her mother's rambling, but it didn't matter. They were together.

The small Catholic Church looked much the same as he remembered it. The flower garden that bordered the walkway to the entrance was in bloom. It was as if the small church had been spared through some kind of Divine providence and protection.

"Other churches hadn't been so fortunate," Peter thought to himself. "All houses of worship weren't created equal, especially Synagogues. God's divine protection apparently didn't apply to them. But then, errant bombs were not necessary in such cases. Just a match and some petrol."

The doors to the Rectory opened and Father Thomas embraced Peter as though he was a long, lost son. The priest poured two cups of strong tea. Settling back into his desk chair, Father Thomas's countenance changed from a welcoming smile to a more solemn look of concern.

"Peter, I won't ask you how you are. You are like all the others fighting our Fuhrer's war. My great sorrow is how the church has failed you—failed everyone."

Peter sipped his tea and looked at the priest. "Even the Jews?"

"Especially the Jews," Father Thomas replied, his face becoming flushed.

Peter held his cup out for the priest to pour more tea. "These days those words could get you arrested or worse."

The priest offered Peter a forlorn smile. "Before you left three years ago, you were a bright young man of integrity who possessed an open mind. Does that still hold true three years later?"

Peter leaned back on the small sofa and stared at the ceiling. "I'm not so bright anymore and my integrity—let's just say war has a way of redefining what it means, if it means anything. I suppose my mind is open . . . primarily open to survival by whatever is required."

Peter returned his gaze to Father Thomas. "Needless to say, I'm not the same boy you knew three years ago nor I'm guessing, are you the same man. I no longer have much use for God and even less for Chaplains unless they can shoot straight."

The priest leaned forward in his chair. "As I said, my great sorrow is how the Church—how I have failed you and our nation and especially, the Jews. You speak of Chaplains, are there even any Chaplains left who believe in Jesus the Christ?"

"I suppose there are a few," Peter shrugged, "but they keep mostly quiet about their personal beliefs since as you know, official policy proclaims the Fuhrer to be our Messiah."

Peter lit a cigarette and offered one to Father Thomas. "There are a few good chaplains. The good ones help out where they can with the wounded, last rites and such. Some shoot better than they pray."

Peter exhaled a stream of smoke. "Of course, most of them aren't like you or Pastor Kempler. They refer to themselves not as Catholics or Lutherans, but as 'German Christians.'"

Father Thomas poured the last of the tea into his and Peter's cups. "Ah, yes. 'Positive Christianity', a thin disguise for a national religion with the Fuhrer as Pope or perhaps more accurately, as you said—Messiah."

The Priest folded his hands together. "Under a just God, the Church doesn't deserve to survive. We can only hope for mercy. None has failed more than mine. We have been more interested in following the example of Caiaphas than of Jesus in accommodating Caesar rather than in standing for Christ. There are a few exceptions like Bonhoeffer and Niemoller and their advocacy for a 'confessional church', which follows the God of the scriptures not the delusions of a Fuhrer."

Peter ground his cigarette butt out in the ashtray. "Franz told me they had both been sent to concentration camps—an unfortunate reward for their faith."

Father Thomas grew quiet, a mask of sorrow shading his face.

Rubbing his eyes, the priest looked at his hands. "Franz used to write me. When his letters quit coming, I feared he had been killed. I was hoping against hope that you would tell me that my fears were unfounded."

"Your fears are not unfounded," Peter replied. "He was killed."

"A Russian bullet, no doubt," Father Thomas sighed.

Peter rubbed the stubble on his chin. "Not a Russian bullet. A German bullet."

The Priest's hand came to his face in shock. "Oh my, did poor Franz take his own life?"

"Major Heinrich shot him," Peter replied. "Franz refused to participate in setting fire to a barn full of Jews so the Major shot him."

Father Thomas began to rock back and forth. "Franz, my dear Franz. Your life held so much promise. You had a heart as well as a mind for theology. Had you not been pressured by your father and infernal family tradition, he would . . . you might still be alive."

The Priest rubbed his temple. "Franz was a spirit too gentle and righteous for this cruel world."

Peter sat on a small bench in the front yard and waited for Anna and her mother to finish packing the picnic that he and Anna were to enjoy on a hill in a cemetery above Hamburg. It had long been a favorite rendezvous for teenagers in love, far away from the prying eyes of their parents and other disapproving elders. Peter heard on a radio broadcast that there was heavy fighting along the Mius River. After Operation Citadel had been called off, he had received his leave while his unit was sent to the rear for a brief rest and refitting.

"Here, Anna, take this bratwurst as well," Frau Rader said as she slipped the morsel wrapped in cheese cloth into the picnic basket. "Compliments of Herr Bittman."

"Herr Bittman," Anna muttered under her breath as she and Peter walked toward the cemetery.

Peter shifted the picnic basket to his other hand. "You don't seem pleased by Herr Bittman's generosity."

Anna looked straight ahead and ignored Peter's remark. Wiping a bead of sweat from her brow, she looked up at the sun, which would soon set. "This has to be one of the hottest and driest summers I can remember."

"It will be cooler above the cemetery under shade of the big oaks," Peter replied.

Patting Peter's rump, Anna laughed, "maybe, maybe not."

The bratwurst, pumpernickel bread and cold strudel made for a fine picnic. When they finished the small jar of apple brandy, Peter lay back on the quilt and Anna snuggled in the crook of his arm.

"Looks like we will have some stars tonight," Peter said, stroking Anna's hair.

Anna looked up at the coming night sky. "I wish those stars could take us away from here . . . to a quiet place with flowers and children playing and plenty to eat and no air-raid sirens."

Peter lit a cigarette. "That's quite a list." He wondered what Werner, Erich and Theo were wishing for tonight.

Anna nuzzled Peter's neck with small, wet kisses and touched him. He knew what she wanted. It was all he used to think about when he was with her before the war. Now, it was different—not completely, but still not the same. Before, Anna's touch had been electric. Now one's lust for survival was stronger than one's sexual desire. Surviving a battle often proved to be the ultimate aphrodisiac, a brief, euphoric burst of pure joy and relief bonding him and his comrades together. Then like spent lovers, they would descend into a bone-numbing weariness that only sleep no matter how brief or fitful, could provide them with any comfort.

There was no way for Anna to know that soldiers on the battlefront did not make love. Sexual liaisons, if they occurred at all, were happenstance. Such intimacies were fleeting and unpredictable, even snatched on occasion from unwilling victims like the time he and Franz were foraging for food.

An armored troop carrier had stopped in the middle of the road thirty yards from them. The hatch opened and a young, frightened, half-naked girl was tossed from the vehicle. When the Grenadiers saw Peter and Franz, they laughed, pointed at the crying girl and gave a thumbs up as if they were on a holiday. The young girl was a whimpering mess. Franz shouted obscenities at the crew as they left in a cloud of dust and tried to comfort the girl. She would have none of it, running from him for the safety of the forest. He called out to her to no avail. He was, after all, a German soldier and to her way of knowing, all Germans were alike.

As Anna's hand and kisses coaxed and encouraged him, Peter recalled one other occasion when a woman in the Ukraine with dancing eyes seduced him . . . or did he seduce her? He could only remember that he had too much local wine. There was music and dancing, and a momentary celebration of life rather than death. Of course, that was in the beginning when the German army was cheered and viewed as liberators. Now they were viewed as little more than Bolshevik oppressors in German disguise.

"Peter," Anna moaned. Then, he remembered what to do.

They lay on the quilt in each other's arms. "The stars are out," Anna mused as she stroked Peter's arm.

"That, they are," Peter replied, kissing the top of her head.

"Peter."

"Yes, Anna."

"Herr Bittman makes me do things."

Peter lit a cigarette. "What kind of things?"

"Mother and I were hungry and he told her to send me by his butcher shop . . . that he had a nice soup bone for us. In the meat locker, he tried to put his hand up my dress."

Peter looked at Anna. "What did you do?"

Anna sat up abruptly. "I slapped him."

"What did he do?" Peter replied.

Anna teared up. "He took back the soup bone."

"I see," Peter replied softly.

"Mother was very cross with me. I couldn't tell her what happened. Herr Bittman is married to her cousin."

Anna buried her face in Peter's chest. "Our hunger began to frighten us. There was never enough to eat. One day I decided to return to Herr Bittman's butcher shop. Every Friday, he gives me a bit of meat and cheese for Mother and me and I. . ."

Anna began to cry. "I'm sorry, Peter."

Peter stroked Anna's hair. "It's alright. You did what you had to do for you and your mother to survive. War changes people, takes the lease off civility and allows the predators to come out during the day. I will talk to Herr Bittman before I leave."

"Mother can't know," Anna replied, drying her eyes on the edge of the quilt. "I don't think it will do any good. Herr Bittman's a greedy and vulgar man."

Peter continued to stroke her hair. "We'll see, Anna. We'll see."

They took in the surroundings from their perch on the hill one last time before the air raid sirens started. Searchlights beamed powerful shafts of light up into the night sky as the roar of Lancaster bombers and the explosions of flack guns made their presence known. Peter and Anna stood frozen in each other's embrace and beheld Hamburg's Armageddon.

Wooden houses were little more than dry kindling for the bombs, shooting flames high into the night sky like Roman candles. The fires quickly joined into a storm of heat and flames, hurling tornado winds 1500 feet upward and outward, sucking the oxygen out of cellars and bomb shelters and peoples' lungs. Tops of trees bent down under weight of the relentless heat. Asphalt streets burst into flames. The harbor and canals ignited in a cascading wall of flames from the fuel oil of damaged and destroyed ships and barges. People ran about frantically, their hair on fire. Flaming horses galloped helter-skelter through the streets. Others ran for safety, only to be tossed about like dry leaves by the firestorm's winds, pulling them back into the heart of the fire. Heat-scorched throats could utter no sound . . . only silence in the midst of wind and flames. The next day would find groups of 4 and 5 corpses—whole families—fused together in death's charcoaled sculptures.

Anna and Peter looked on in horror, wondering if anyone caught up in the inferno below could possibly survive. They spent the night on the hill. Anna could no longer bear to watch and returned to the quilt. Peter remained transfixed by the consuming fire that turned the old German city of Hamburg into a smoldering ash-heap, a remnant of what hell must look like. He could hear Anna crying and knew he should go to her, but he couldn't pull himself away from the scene below. He thought he had seen everything on the Eastern front, more than enough fire and smoke and death and dying. But this was something else . . . in the blink of an eye what was, was no more . . . not a drawn-out battle of heaving armies trying to annihilate one another, but a sudden event, a silent, consuming whisper of destruction. Peter sat in reverent silence throughout the night meditating on what the end of the world looked like. What were he, Erich, Werner, and Theo fighting for? What was there to come home to?

Peter said his goodbyes to Frau Rader and Anna with the promise that he would return for Anna, that they would make a life together after the war. He partly meant it and in some ways he didn't. Who could know if he or Anna would be there when the war ended, but then she knew that as well as he did. Peter wasn't even sure he wanted to marry Anna or anyone else for that matter. Still, he made the promise because he saw the wish in her eyes. Sometimes a wish is enough in times such as these.

Father Thomas had perished in the fire along with the pile of rubble where his church had once stood. Peter assumed that the divine protection which had previously spared the beautiful church and courtyard was needed more elsewhere.

As fate would have it, while Father Thomas and his church were no more, Herr Bittman and his butcher shop were spared. The butcher greeted Peter when he entered the shop.

"Herr Steiner, are you returning to the front?"

Peter nodded.

"You brave lads are doing a magnificent job in stemming the Bolshevik threat."

Holding up several sausages, Bittman continued. "Perhaps, a sausage and some cheese and bread for your journey?"

Peter nodded once more.

Herr Bittman wrapped the food and reached out to hand the parcel to Peter over the counter. "I must say, you are a man of few words."

In one movement, Peter's left hand took the parcel of food from Bittman's outstretched hand and with his right hand, he drove his dagger through Bittman's palm, pining it to the counter.

Bittman screamed in pain.

Peter placed his index finger on Bittman's lips and the butcher moaned in obedience.

"Herr Bittman, although your hand will heal, there are two things you must do to stay alive. First, you must see than Anna and Frau Rader are provided by you each week with a good cut of whatever meat you have available. Second, you must never touch Anna again. If you don't provide them with meat or if you touch Anna, I will kill you. Are my terms clear to you?"

Herr Bittman sputtered, "But I . . ."

Peter once again placed his finger against Bittman's lips. "No need to speak. Simply nod if you understand and agree to my terms."

When Bittman nodded, Peter pulled his dagger from the butcher's hand and wiped it clean on Herr Bittman's apron. He returned his dagger to the scabbard attached to his belt, picked up the parcel and left the shop.

Peter looked at the troops milling around the train station. If he could catch the next transport, he could be back with Werner, Erich and Theo within seventy-two hours—maybe sooner. He had heard the fighting on the Mius front was heavy and that Hill 213 was a bear. His friends would enjoy the taste of real sausages and cheese. He smiled at the thought of it.

12

Leningrad Lullaby

THE LUTWAFFE LEFT WITH a roar. Except for the pop and crackle of burning buildings, the hard-packed snow swept an eerie silence over the landscape. A full moon caressed the wounded city, illuminating bodies lying about like discarded paper dolls. Some were dead, others dying—calling out in the cold darkness for their mothers.

The "all clear" whistle sounded and what remained of Leningrad slowly came up for air. Dark, stooped figures shuffled out from the broken ruins and shelters onto the streets. Soldiers evaluated the damage while medics moved toward the cries of the maimed and mangled. Women followed, pulling sleds piled with rags which passed for bandages and blankets.

Two women, one who had seen better years and the other, little more than a girl, covered another body

Martina trudged alongside Katya. "You want me to help you pull the sled?"

The young girl shook her head as she surveyed the carnage. "Not many survivors tonight."

Martina shrugged and pulled the woolen scarf more tightly around her head and neck. "They're the lucky ones. At least they won't die a slow death of starvation and disease like the rest of us."

Kneeling down to examine another body, Katya gave her companion an exasperated look. "Don't talk like that, Martina. Life is still precious."

The older woman coughed. "Precious to who? Only to the young ones like you, dear Katya, who don't know any better. You may dream of a future. All I dream of is a bowl of hot cabbage soup."

Katya stood up and smiled. "Look what I found!"

"What is it?" Martina asked impatiently, stamping her feet against the cold.

"Well, it's not a bowl of cabbage soup, but a piece of bread is the next best thing," Katya replied, extending her found treasure toward her friend.

Martina's eyes flickered at Katya's offering as she grabbed the young girl's hand and pushed it into the folds of her shawl.

"Turn your back to the street and cover our dead benefactor with blankets. Others will be watching. A piece of bread could cost us what's left of our miserable lives."

Katya did as she was told. The two women knelt around the body and slowly ate the bread, savoring each morsel.

Rising to their feet, they made their way to the next group of bodies. As Katya struggled to pull the small sled over a patch of debris, she heard Martina moan. Freeing the sled, Katya hurried toward her friend.

Martina gestured for Katya to stop. "Don't come any closer. Look away, Katya. Look away."

Katya pushed past the older woman, drawn as the young always are, toward what is forbidden. She stood frozen at the sight before her. Like a bizarre collection of eviscerated puzzle pieces that used to be human, a charred torso and head lay in a bloody heap next to the burning timbers of a collapsed building. An arm was where a leg should have been and a soldier's cap perched on what was left of a hand.

Martina sighed wearily and clasped her hands together. "When you think you've seen it all, you haven't. There's always something more."

Shaking her head, she gently squeezed Katya's shoulder. "Come, child. At least this one's suffering is over."

The two women stood motionless as a tiny slit where a mouth once was opened and replied with a soft, hoarse whisper, "Not yet."

13

The Man Who Loved Potatoes

HE LOVED POTATOES. BAKED, boiled or mashed, all he needed was butter, salt and pepper. On special occasions, He prepared his personal favorite, scalloped potatoes made with cream, cheese, flour, onions and even a bit of garlic.

Since his wife died, he lived alone on his small farm, tending the garden, orchard, chickens and Rose, his milk cow. When the Germans came, life became more difficult. Although things could have been better, he remained grateful. His garden kept him busy and his dog, Jules, kept him company.

Given his gastronomic affinity for potatoes, they were in one form or another, the entrée for each evening meal. A hearty supper was followed by an evening walk, a full pipe and warm fire enjoyed by Jules and him until bedtime. Then a page or two from the Good Book and a short prayer signaled the end of another day.

Each day his routine followed the same pattern—just the way he liked it. Until the morning he entered the barn to milk Rose and found a wounded American pilot.

The Germans would be looking for him. Had his nosey neighbor, Pierre, who lived down the lane caught sight of him? He wished the American had picked another barn. Truth be told, he wanted him to leave his place of relative calm and freedom. That's when Father Francis's homily from last Sunday came to him, the one that commanded him to care for the stranger and the one who was in need. Given the present circumstance, it was a message he didn't want to hear or remember.

Then the American stood up and spoke his name, "Peter."

The wounded pilot didn't know any French and he didn't know any English.

With a tip of his hat, he slowly approached the American and with Jules leading the way, helped him to his house. After cleaning and bandaging the American's wound, he did for him what he did best. He served him a nice plate of boiled potatoes, cooked in butter with leeks, properly salted and peppered along with a piece of bread and a glass of Bordeaux. Although he was something of an artist when it came to cooking potatoes, he had never seen anyone relish each mouthful the way the American did. Each spoonful brought a groan of culinary satisfaction and a fresh smile to his face. Sopping up the plate's scattered remnants, his guest popped the last bit of bread in his mouth and bowed in appreciation.

That night the farmer slept little, pondering what his next move might be. The sound of a Wehrmacht military transport at first light answered the question.

The long and short of it was that Peter was questioned by the Germans and sent to a Prisoner of War camp and he was sent to the local police station to be interrogated. The village folk knew him well, including Pierre and the other collaborators, so it became clear soon enough that he wasn't part of the Resistance, just a widower who lived alone on a small farm with his dog and milk cow. Of course, the Germans as was their nature, preferred to err on the side of safety rather than mercy. Jules went to Father Francis, Rose, the chickens and the title of his farm went to the local orphanage.

The next morning, his back against a pock-marked wall in the courtyard, he stood facing a firing squad. As they raised their rifles, he closed his eyes and wondered if there would be potatoes in heaven.

14

A Pair of Boots

IT WAS A PLEASANT enough October afternoon. Oompah music reverberated through the crowd of revelers drinking beer and eating warm pretzels.

The old man looked at his fifty-year-old son sitting across the table from him with sad, hollow eyes.

"Erwin, the gulag they sent us to when we surrendered was a place beyond hope. We did what we could to survive though few of us did. Bitter cold and hunger. Some gave up like in Stalingrad. They invited a bullet from the guards or embraced a frozen sleep. In fact, the greatest regret of my life occurred at Gulag 17."

The old man took another sip of beer and seemed to slip back into a dark place he had been struggling against since the war.

"Hans was sick. Working in the forests all day without enough to eat did him in like many others. When he caught pneumonia, there was little hope for him."

"Father, is that the same Hans you grew up with?"

"Yes, Hans was my best friend before and during the war."

After paying the waiter, the two men drank deeply from the fresh steins of beer. Wiping his mouth with the back of his shirtsleeve, the old man continued.

"I could see the others staring at Hans. I knew what they were thinking. I was thinking the same thing. It wouldn't be long before he was finished. It was all a matter of timing. Like anything in life, it's always a matter of timing. Like getting to the morning soup line. Those who were too anxious, who got to there too early, were harassed and often beaten by the guards. Sometimes they were beaten so badly they couldn't eat their soup, which meant they were either sent to the infirmary from which most never returned or sent to the forest where they wouldn't have the strength to cut timber. Whether they were shot in the forest or left to die in the infirmary, they died because their timing was all wrong. If you were too late to the soup line, there might be nothing left for you to eat or if there was, it was little more than warm water. Yes, proper timing was essential if you were to survive in the gulag. You must get to the soup line at the right time so as not to get a beating, but not too late when there was little if anything left to eat."

The old man pulled a cigarette from the pocket of his jacket and his son lit it for him. The two men sat in silence, one smoking and the other watching.

"That's how it was with Hans. His timing was all wrong. He was too far back in the work line to get one of the ponchos. He spent too much time cleaning his boots that particular morning. I warned him, but Hans was always stubborn. He got pneumonia because he got wet. He got wet because he was late in line. It's always about the timing."

Erwin rubbed his chin. "Why did Hans spend so much time cleaning his boots? He must have known the risk he was taking."

"Perhaps," his father replied, lighting another cigarette from the butt of the one he had just finished. "But the truth was, Hans had the finest pair of boots in the camp among the inmates. He always managed to keep them oiled and they were even lined with wool. Hans was a genuine craftsman when it came to boots. He was a cobbler's apprentice before the war."

"How do you think Hans got the wool to line his boots?"

Erwin looked at his father quizzically, "I don't know."

"He repaired the guards' boots, including the Commandant's. From time to time, they would reward him with a piece of bread or a bit of oil or a remnant from a wool blanket.

As I was saying, Hans was dying. He knew it as we all did. And I know it sounds gruesome, but we all wanted his boots—every one of us. As his best friend, he had promised them to me. Still, it was a matter of timing. We all watched and waited."

The old man was aware of the disconcerted look in his son's eyes.

"Yes, even me, his best friend. Like vultures, we circled his body, waiting for him to draw his last breath.

I could hear the others shuffling around, talking among themselves in heavy, desperate whispers, waiting for the right time. Hans' body was still. I wasn't sure if he was dead or asleep. All eyes were on me as I touched his leg. He didn't move. I needed those boots. Hans would never take off his boots for more than a few minutes. He even slept with them on. As you can imagine, good boots were a high priority in the gulag. Frozen feet meant frostbite which like so many other things meant death.

Finally, I could stand it no longer. I began to pull the boot off Hans' left leg. He groaned. I stopped for a moment, frozen in shame and backed away. I could feel the stares of the others. May God forgive me. I pulled off his boots anyway. As I wrestled with his other boot, Hans slowly turned his head and looked at me."

Erwin's look had changed from one of consternation to one of horror.

"How did he look at you father?"

The old man took another long drink from his stein.

"He looked at me in a way I can't explain—in a way I can't forget.

After I pulled off both boots, I backed away clutching them tightly to my chest. Then the others, as if on cue, took what was left. I stood next to my bunk weeping. When they had finished with Hans, he was shivering naked in the cold. I could feel his eyes on me one last time. His body shuddered twice and he let out one last gasping breath, then died. I walked over to him. He was quiet.

His eyes were closed. A tear streaked his left cheek. I had taken by force what he had promised as a gift."

Erwin reached over and placed his hand on his father's.

"Father, it was a terrible time. People did whatever it took to survive."

"I know Erwin. I know better than most. But Hans was my friend. A few minutes more would have made all the difference. A few minutes more would have made a robbery a generous gift."

Father and son once again sat in silence, one wondering if he should have never asked the question and the other wondering if he should have ever answered it. When Erwin called to the waiter for a final round, the old man's thoughts were drawn once again to those boots. And in spite himself, in spite of his shame and sorrow, a slow, guilty smile spread across his ancient, wrinkled face.

15

The Clock Maker

Sound was the first thing Walt Murphy became aware of when he entered Aldo Romer's modest brownstone. Tick Tock. Tick Tock. The three antique clocks precisely positioned on the fireplace mantle signaled the passing of time.

Meticulous was the word that came to mind as the young journalist surveyed his host's small sitting room. The room had a certain Victorian sensibility with its long dark red curtains that framed the large picture window. A small, polished antique writing table sat in the corner. Two ancient, dark brown leather wingback chairs perched on either side of a small, ornate coffee table. Meticulous also applied to the slightly stoop-shouldered 92-year-old man who ushered him to one of the leather chairs. Aldo Romer wore a vintage tweed suit and vest. His bright blue eyes peered through a pair of gold-rimmed glasses perched on the bridge of his nose. Not a hair was out of place and his goatee was trimmed close. When Mr. Romer went to the kitchen to retrieve refreshments, Walt made a mental note that the person he was to interview was a fastidious man given to fine detail.

Walt Murphy complimented his elderly host on the ornate French press that he used to prepare the coffee.

Handing a fresh brewed cup to Walt, Aldo smiled. "Yes, it is an exquisite design created for me at Buchen . . ." Aldo cleared his throat. "The designer in question was a true artisan. I have collected several presses over the years, but this one remains my favorite."

The two men sipped their coffee and munched on gingerbread cookies. Aldo Romer had a certain endearing quality about him. His genial manner and the twinkle of his clear, blue eyes combined with the symmetry of a disciplined smile spoke of a somewhat ambiguous distinction depending upon one's interpretation. His look could be a gesture of relaxed approval or the subtle response of seductive ridicule. Walt Murphy found the ambiguity of Aldo's masked response interesting though not surprising given the fact that Aldo wasn't his real name, but rather a mask of a different sort. The senior citizen drinking coffee and making small talk previously lived in Germany, his country of origin, as Albert Adolphus. To the inmates of the concentration camp where he was an SS physician, he was known as the "Smiling Death."

Walt Murphy placed his cup and saucer on the table in front of him. "Thank you for the coffee and refreshments, Mr. Romer."

"You may call me Aldo," his elderly host replied. "For one who likes his afternoon coffee bold with a clean finish, I have found none better than my favorite custom blend from Vienna."

Walt pulled his notebook and digital recorder from his brief case. "Given your current status, I must confess surprise that you chose to invite me to interview you."

Aldo Romer waved his hands. "No recorder, please. I prefer the old ways. You may write down anything and everything, but no recorder. To answer your question, my reasons are really quite simple. I have fondness for reading several newspapers each day, including the one for which you write. I have found your editorial commentaries to be well written and disciplined and perhaps most importantly, balanced."

Aldo leaned back in his chair. "Mr. Murphy, you are a journalist who is inclined to put your personal feelings aside in order to provide the reader with both sides of an argument. While your writing is incisive and sometimes provocative, it is always clear and within the boundaries of propriety. That kind of discipline and integrity impresses me."

"Still, given that you are in the middle of a deportation hearing for war crimes, why would you grant me an interview that could damage your prospects?"

Aldo chuckled. "My prospects—what prospects, my young friend? At 92, my prospects are less than stellar no matter what the outcome of the hearing. I am confident that I will eventually be deported if I live long enough. Perhaps, I will even stand trial in the Fatherland. Whatever happens is of little matter. I have had my time and Father Time will soon come for me as he eventually does for all of us."

Walt shifted his weight in the chair. "Why an interview?"

Aldo pursed his lips in a moment of contemplation. "Much has been written about me—my past—in the last few months. Some of it is true, some not. What has not been reported is my side of the events that took place during that terrible war. There are one's actions and there are also one's intentions."

Pouring himself another cup of coffee, Aldo continued. "So here we sit, Mr. Murphy. Ask me anything."

Walt opened his notebook. "You've been accused of horrific crimes during the war, including conducting medical experiments on men, women and children at Buchenwald."

Aldo waved off the question. "I will answer that and other charges in due time. To understand such claims, you must first understand something of who I am and what motivated me to do what I did." Aldo took a sip of coffee and pointed at the antique clocks that adorned his wall. "You must understand something of what makes me tick."

The young journalist considered his host's response. "So, what would you like for me to know about—how did you put it—your motivations and intentions?"

The former concentration camp doctor and current clock maker gripped the armrests of his chair and leaned to one side, staring at his favorite antique clock. "I believe in an ordered universe, a universe which desires—no requires—purity and perfection through precision. After the war I escaped to Spain for two years. During that time, I fell into an abyss of despair, doubting my purpose and very being. I asked myself what had I done? What had I become? I drank heavily and even contemplated ending what was left of my life."

Aldo's countenance softened. "As I drew closer to that dark appointed hour where I would exit my pitiful existence, I decided to go outside for one last look at the night sky. I always like the pristine brilliance of a star-filled night sky. And then it happened."

"What happened?" Walt asked.

Aldo's eyes grew moist with excitement. "Through that bright, shining star-lit sky which illuminated the encroaching darkness, the universe spoke to me."

"Spoke to you?"

"Yes, my young friend, I know what I am saying sounds a bit preposterous. Yet, call it what you will, it penetrated my despair with an epiphany of sorts. A revelation as terrible as the means on occasion may be, are sometimes justified by the ends—the greater good that is served. A measure of salvation was revealed to me in that darkest of moments that while some of my actions may have been deplorable, my intentions still held some hope of virtue. What motivated me in the deepest part of my being was to improve humanity. After that life-changing experience, I eventually found my way to America and became a clock maker. I earned my living by designing, refurbishing, and repairing antique clocks. I made them operate as they were created to perform."

Aldo clasped his hands together and grew pensive. "Clocks are an amazing invention. No longer does one have to look at the position of the sun against the horizon to estimate the time of day. The clock allows us to go about our day's chores and our night's activities in an efficient and purposeful manner. Of course, such an observation only holds true if the clock operates as it was designed. The mechanics of weight-driven clocks are fascinating. The gravitational pull of carefully crafted weights, the acoustic construction of the cabinet and the hammer and rods produce a distinct sound—the sound of time and life passing."

The old man pointed to a tall, elegant grandfather clock occupying the corner of the room. "That is a 16-hammer clock with a triple chime that on every hour sounds an exquisite rendering of Beethoven's Ninth Symphony. Working on old clocks is both an art and a science. When the clock doesn't perform as it was intended, it is useless. The faulty part, be it a cog or a spring or other component, must be discarded if it cannot be repaired. In such an instance, I must conceive, engineer, and create a new part with the correct tolerance and performance characteristics to make the clock function as it was designed to do."

Walt Murphy put down his pen and folded his hands across his lap. "The law is more interested in one's actions than intentions. Judgment is rendered on what a person actually does. As the old saying goes, 'actions speak louder than words—and perhaps, intentions.' There aren't any war crimes against experimenting with broken clocks, but broken and discarded lives—that's another matter."

Aldo's brow furrowed as he toyed with his goatee. "Of course, I lived under German law which is more sensitive to one's intentions than your legal system. And you are correct in what you say. The epiphany was mine and no one else's. Still, the ways and laws of the universe are not the ways and laws of humankind. Early in my studies at the university many years ago, I experienced another revelation, an intense awareness that the universe itself chose to evolve over time through a great drama towards perfection, especially perfection of the human species. Call it nature's engineering if you wish or perhaps, the great Clockmaker in the sky, but the process as Darwin recognized was in accordance with the grand design of the universe itself. That particular revelation led me into a labyrinth where science, medical practice, and ethics converge in what is often an uneasy alliance. My personal intentions were not totally in keeping with the Reich's dogma. While it is true, I believed at the time that the Aryan race which produced the Bach's and Hegel's of the world was superior to other races, I bore no personal animosity toward other races, including Jews and Slavs."

Walt stopped writing once more and looked at the old man sitting across from him. "You speak of Bach and Hegel. What about the Einstein's, Tolstoy's, and Freud's of the world?"

Aldo adjusted his glasses and nodded. "You make a valid point, Mr. Murphy. I grant you that other races have their outbursts of genius. Yet, I would suggest that such individuals, while no doubt make exceptional contributions, may be to some extent, anomalies."

Walt arched his eyebrow. "Do you still hold such beliefs?"

Aldo Romer flicked a piece of lint off his vest. "I must confess that over the years, I have moderated my thinking a bit. There is no question as a young, idealistic physician I became caught up in the resurgence of a distraught Fatherland and the charisma of its leader. As an old man, I am more circumspect and even a bit skeptical of charismatic politicians and public leaders. While I am less susceptible to idealistic naiveté than when I was a young man, I am just as convinced that the order of the universe requires—even demands—the pursuit of perfection and purity. To that end, my actions, while perhaps unacceptable by today's legal and ethical standards, were motivated by a genuine desire to perfect our species toward the improvement of all humankind."

The young journalist's skepticism was obvious. "But you, a physician, conducted medical experiments which resulted in the deaths of innocent Jewish, Slav and other men, women and children. They suffered terribly at your hand."

Aldo demonstrated little obvious emotion as he shifted in his chair. "Guilty as charged. My actions are what they were by today's standards, perhaps even unforgivable. But my intentions—my intentions were motivated by a higher calling, a fervent desire to perfect my race and our species."

Walt observed Aldo Romer pouring himself a glass of water. He was still meticulous, but there was something else—something missing. It was as if his mind was agile enough to convince himself if no one else, that his intentions, imaginary or real, somehow justified what he actually did. Walt wasn't sure, but there was a sense that no matter how keen Aldo's intellect was, there was a lack of balance—an emptiness or void where his heart should be.

Aldo took a long drink before continuing. "As I noted before, unlike many of my party comrades, I held no personal animosity toward Jews, or for that matter, Slavs. Because one believes his race to be superior, doesn't mean he holds other races to be of no value or worth. Yes, I was motivated to improve and perfect the Aryan race. My assumption was that other races would inevitably benefit from such efforts as well. Still, as you say, regardless of my zeal, ideological naiveté, and good intentions, innocent people were sacrificed."

Walt poured himself a glass of water. "You refer to it as sacrifice. I would call it murder."

"I'm certain you and your justice system do. Life is often unfair and capricious. Unfortunately, pain and suffering are often the price of progress. You might consider the fate of Native Americans or even the Orientals who died building your railroads westward, or perhaps, even your own Japanese citizens who were held in internment camps. As unfair as the march of progress can be, the greater good also has to be considered. Sometimes, the end does, in fact, justify the means. The universe more often than not, exacts a high price from us as we move toward a more perfect state of being."

Walt Murphy could feel a headache coming on. "While I am no philosopher or legal practitioner, I would hold to the point that on a legal and more importantly, a moral level, it is still murder. I would also venture a further conclusion. While I don't claim to fathom the purpose or mind of the universe, your assumption of its requirement for the unbridled pursuit of purity and perfection seems to me to be a kind of fool's gold."

Aldo's ears perked up. "Fool's gold . . . interesting. Why do say that?"

Walt closed his notebook. "That's right. Fool's gold. As a physician and as a clock maker, you have been focused on the parts. You have to some extent, excused your actions based upon your perception of the purity of your intentions. You and I and all other human beings, regardless of race, have pretty much the same parts. But we are more than that. We are more than the sum of our parts. Bach composed incredible music, but you, Mr. Romer—Mr. Adolphus, you contributed to the greatest symphony of the murder of innocents that the world has ever seen."

Beethoven's Ninth began. "Ah, Mr. Murphy, our time for today is up. You see, I have a dinner engagement this evening with my lawyer. We could meet again tomorrow if you like."

Walt Murphy folded his notebook and placed it in his leather satchel. "Yes, I would like to learn more about your work and those you worked with. Context is important to me when writing a story like yours."

"Indeed, Mr. Murphy, indeed. Same time tomorrow?"

Walt nodded in agreement. "Same time tomorrow."

Walt parked his vintage VW Beetle in front of the old brownstone covered with ivy. Three crows perched on a power line watched him as he walked up the short flight of steps and rang Aldo's doorbell. Their cackling chorus seemed ominous in a strange sort of way, a grim testimony of what was past and what was to come.

The door opened and there stood Aldo, immaculately attired in a cashmere navy blazer, gray flannel slacks and a pale blue silk tie.

"Walter, as I expected, you are right on time. Come in, come in."

Nobody ever called Walt, Walter. Once in the sixth grade, Johnny Spoletti did, but after a brief, surprise encounter in the alleyway on the way home after school, Johnny came to understand that Walt's proper name was 'Walt.' Instinctively Walt considered correcting Aldo, but then thought the better of it. What was the point in correcting Herr Romer. He was old school prim and proper. Besides, he was there to find some morsel of truth, if possible, not alienate his host.

Aldo Romer handed Walt a glass of Scotch and settled into his wing back chair in front of the fireplace. "Given that today's meeting is close to the five o'clock hour, I thought, perhaps, a cocktail rather than coffee might be in order. I allow myself a single glass of whiskey each day at this time. I have found over the years that a well-seasoned single malt Scotch is more suited to my palate than Schnapps."

Aldo raised his glass to Walt. "As the English are fond of saying, 'Cheers.'"

The two men drank in silence for several moments, each gathering his thoughts.

Placing his half-empty tumbler on a coaster, Aldo looked at Walt and smiled. "So, my young friend, where should we start our conversation today?"

Walt shuffled through his notes. "I would like to know more about the specifics of the experiments you and others were engaged in. Are you familiar with Karl Gebhardt and his protégé, Herta Oberheuser and their experiments subjecting prisoners to traumatic wounds? I have a note somewhere that you and Ms. Oberheuser may have been briefly acquainted."

Aldo's twinkling eyes offered the hint of a smile. "I am impressed, Walter, with both the depth of your research and the delicate manner in which you allude to the nature of my and Herta's relationship."

Taking a sip of whiskey, Aldo continued. "Herta and I met during a seminar in Berlin. Our attraction to each other was mutual so we went on holiday together once—I believe it was Vienna in the springtime. She was a handsome enough woman, though quite needy."

The old man smiled to himself. "A neediness that I must admit, served me quite well that weekend."

Walt opened his notebook. "What about Gebhardt and the experiments?"

"Gebhardt," Aldo replied dismissively, "was a stubborn, vain fool. He was skilled in what you Americans call schmoozing. He managed to schmooze his way into being Himmler's personal physician. Because of that, he received promotions when he should have received a court-martial. He was anti-science, almost medieval in his philosophy of medical treatment. Many of us felt he was complicit in Reinhard Heydrich's death for refusing to treat his wounds with Sulfamonides, a new synthetic antibiotic that was available. He nearly killed poor Speer as well."

Walt stopped writing and looked at Aldo "And the experiments?"

"Yes, the experiments. Although gruesome as you might imagine, they were necessary and hold some degree of virtue in that they advanced the treatment of our soldiers' traumatic war wounds with synthetic antibiotics such as Sulfamonide. Soldiers lived who would have otherwise died. The world has in fact, benefited from the development of those drugs, including American soldiers."

"Polish prisoners and children died excruciating deaths as a result of those experiments. There was a report that Ms. Oberheuser rubbed broken glass and sawdust into their wounds," Walt replied.

"Yes, yes, no doubt they did suffer great pain. And yes, the wounds were induced to mimic actual battlefield wounds. One thing about Herta, she wasn't the least bit squeamish in her pursuit of results and meeting her superior's expectations."

Aldo grew quiet as watched the blue flames dance along his gas logs. "Poor Herta. After she was released from prison, a Ravensbruck survivor recognized her and her medical license was rescinded. It seems a shame. She had served her time in prison and needed a means of supporting herself."

"What about those persons she maimed who survived the war? What means of support were they entitled to?"

Aldo looked from the fire to Walt, a weary, yet defiant flash shadowed his eyes. "Your point is taken. Most survivors were compensated by the German government, but of course, how can one who has suffered so much be adequately compensated? The circumstances of life are often unfair and the rigorous demands of scientific truth can no doubt, be harsh."

Walt ran his hand through his hair. "I believe your primary 'scientific' work was at Buchenwald. Tell me about that."

Aldo's quizzical look confirmed that Walt's edge of sarcasm did not go unnoticed.

Rising from his chair, Aldo reached for the whiskey decanter. "I believe an exception is in order to my rule of one drink. Another dollop of single malt might do us both a bit of good."

"My—our—work addressed a range of combat related issues. There were experiments that focused on phosphorous burns from incendiary devices. You might want to read about the Dresden firebombing raid for a more in-depth understanding of the effects of such wounds. Others worked on the effects of poisons. There were also efforts to understand bone, muscle, and nerve damage as well as the effects of gangrene. Oh yes, and there were experiments which studied the effects of freezing such as when pilots were shot down in the north Atlantic. All of these experiments required the use of men, women and children, most of whom died agonizing deaths."

"Not all, but yes, most of the work required human subjects, many of whom did not survive," Aldo replied with a shrug. "Of course, many more prisoners died as a result of the camp commandant and his unstable wife's decisions."

"They would be the Koch's," Walt replied, looking at his notes. "So, you knew as you put it, 'his unstable wife', who was referred to by the camp inmates as the 'Witch of Buchenwald'?"

"Everyone knew Ilse Koch. The prisoners gave her that name. We thought of her more as the 'Whore of Buchenwald'."

"Why?" Walt queried.

"Let's just say that her excesses were evident when she had an extravagant indoor sports area built. Of course, her preferred sport was of a sexual nature and not a discriminating one at that. She apparently enjoyed a frequent and varied clientele that rumor had it, included Jewish prisoners. Waldemar Hoven, the Chief Medical Officer, was one of her many lovers. He apparently couldn't get enough of her. He even gave an SS officer who was set to testify against Frau Koch a lethal injection. He only escaped execution because by 1945 there was a severe shortage of doctors. Of course, that fortuitous circumstance only delayed the inevitable. He was convicted at Nuremberg and hanged in 1948."

"In the west, most women involved in the death camps escaped execution. Many weren't even brought to trial. Illse Koch was one of the few women tried for war crimes who died in prison. In the east, the tribunals were less forgiving. Trials and executions were much more frequent."

Aldo drummed his fingers on the arm of his chair. "Though impervious to the greater good and driven by her desires, she was a consummate actress. I will give her that."

The old man smiled. "Of course, her respite was only temporary. I understand that she hung herself at Aichau Prison. I suppose the Grim Reaper comes for each of us at the appointed time."

Walt chewed on the end of his pen. "Your experiments focused more on chemical and biological warfare, including plagues such as typhus, cholera and smallpox."

Aldo swirled the ice around in his whiskey glass. "Yes, that was my primary area of study. I would agree with Kurt Blome's testimony at the 'doctors' trials' that our focus was on defensive tactics against biological weapons and attacks. As the eastern front deteriorated, rumors abounded regarding the Bolsheviks' potential for chemical and biological attacks."

Rising from his chair Walt walked over to the fireplace and warmed his hands. "You offer an interesting rationale, especially given that there is ample evidence that the Wehrmacht's Science Section supported the use of chemical and biological weapons against England, the United States, and the Soviet Union. I believe it was referred to as 'Blitzableiter' or 'Lightening Rod.' Seventeen hundred prisoners died as a result of those experiments."

Reaching for his glass of Scotch, Aldo's eyes narrowed almost imperceptibly. "I wasn't directly associated with that work. It took place at Mauthasen . I heard rumors about plans for nerve gas to be dropped from airplanes, but remember, in 1944 times were growing desperate in the Fatherland. You might also recall that Blome was acquitted."

After taking a long drink, he continued. "As I am sure you are already aware, Karl Genzken was my superior officer at Buchenwald from 1941 through 1945. During that time period, we developed and tested the effects of vaccines for typhus, smallpox and cholera. Were our acts immoral? In hindsight, I can accept that while my intentions were good, many of the acts themselves were unethical. Were they illegal? No. In fact, we were ordered by our leaders to conduct the experiments to help with the treatment of our wounded and as a defensive measure against attacks from our enemies. Of course, history has taught us that when a war is over, the victors not the vanquished decide what is ethical and legal."

Walt rubbed the stubble on his chin. "I have one last question for you. I keep getting this nagging feeling that you and the other doctors understood that the prisoners were human on some level, but never really saw them as human beings. It is hard for me to get past that—that no matter what your orders or intentions were, how could you do what you did to innocent men, women and children?"

Aldo clasped his hands together and studied them before responding. "What you say we did is in many ways unbelievable. And yet, we were taught that the Jews had caused our suffering and were themselves a dangerous contagion bent on destroying us. We were taught that the Slavs were subhuman and the Bolshevik horde was a threat to our very existence. We were a desperate and hungry people, the scourge of the west with no hope until the Fuhrer emerged. He willed a rebirth that we, not the Jews, were the chosen people. In hindsight, our new-found pride in ourselves and our nation led to a kind of collective vanity and arrogance that led to our undoing."

Taking a handkerchief from his pocket, Aldo wiped his upper lip. "In spite of my insensitivity to the humanity of my subjects, the result of bias and prejudice I had been indoctrinated with for ten years prior to the events we are talking about, I did feel more sympathy for their suffering than you might imagine. I did what had to be done for the scientific integrity of my work and not a whit more. I did, in fact, write up official reports on two occasions regarding what I considered acts of sadism by other colleagues. One of those reports resulted in a court-martial and reduction in rank. And while it will sound strange to you, I took every opportunity to end my subject's suffering, on several occasions even risking the validity of critical experimental outcomes. Do my meager efforts pale in comparison to the suffering that was endured by prisoners? Of course. But at the very least, they do indicate that I was connected on some level to the humanity of those who suffered at my hand. On one occasion, I confided in the Camp Chaplain that I had a growing sense of melancholy that what I was doing to them, the prisoners, I was also doing to myself. Still, in the end in spite of any misgivings, I did my duty knowing that after the war, I would be pursued, that in the end, I like everyone else, could not escape my past. Now, it seems my past has come for me."

After draining the last of his Scotch, Walt put his pen in his pocket and closed his notebook. "Mr. Romer, I want to thank you for your time and hospitality. I believe I have all I need to finish the article."

"Will it be fair?"

"I hope so," Walt responded with the most subtle of smiles. "That would certainly be my intention.

16

Johann Wept

TIME CAN OFTEN HEAL wounds both inflicted and received. That's how it seems or is at least, hoped for. Memory has its own way of remembering, rendering a verdict of innocent where guilty is called for. Even when guilt insists on being recognized, time's passing tends to diminish the wounds given as well as their effects. Guilty perhaps, but not as guilty as others, maybe in time, not guilty at all. Still, fragments slither in from one's past, ruining a night's good sleep. Ready or not, they came to Johann. Now, an old man, forgotten time has returned, peering out from the abyss, revealing shadows and faces that he had hoped would be forgotten.

Almost ninety years of age, Johann Hoffner sat and waited while others bustled around him. He had pressed his best three-piece wool suit, meticulously trimmed his moustache and polished his lone pair of dress shoes to a high shine. Checking the time from his grandfather's pocket watch, he took another delicate sip of coffee and surveyed his surroundings.

Since the war, he had done his best to become the man he hoped for in remembrance. He returned to the Lutheran church of his childhood, devout in his intention to redeem the contradictory lessons he had been taught as a boy—love God with all one's heart, mind and soul, but keep a sly, hidden eye out for those who are

different, especially foreigners and Jews. He recalled his SS training officer, himself a former man of the cloth, commenting to him
as a young man that Martin Luther would have liked to nail more
than his ninety-five Theses to the wall.

That was then, when as a young boy in the Hitler Youth, he
was taught that the Jews had infected the Fatherland from within.
That they were both the primary cause and effect of Germany's
decline and defeat in World War I. That the economic catastrophe
that had befallen the Fatherland was because of them and other
corrupt deviants. And there was also his grandfather, a decorated
veteran and ardent supporter of Germany's resurrection under the
Fuhrer. What was a boy to do?

Like many of his peers, he followed his friends in joining the
SS. Why be a regular soldier, a simple hero, when one could become a member of the elite military, a super-hero, instead? Johann
learned soon enough that the glitter and sheen of glory turned dull
in the midst of combat and that dead men don't blow trumpets,
beat drums or march in parades.

After the war, he felt reborn in 1953 when his cousin, Willie,
from his mother's side, sponsored his passage to the United States.
In the land of the free, one was free to breathe and be—become
something new, something better and now unfortunately, this: free
to be pursued by the truth from a distant past.

"Will the Court rise," signaled all who were in attendance
for this auspicious occasion, the deportation trial for one, Johann
Hoffner, to rise to their feet as the Judge entered the courtroom.
Johann steeled himself for a scene he had rehearsed countless
times on nights when sleep had abandoned him. It seemed that
the age of eighty-nine, his day of reckoning had finally arrived.

"SS Untersturmfuhrer Johann Hoffner . . ." the Prosecutor began as he projected an image of a smiling young SS officer version
of the old man sitting at the defendant's table onto the screen.

After recovering from his wounds fighting in France, his
younger self had been reassigned as one of the officers who oversaw
the endless stream of human cargo that poured out of overcrowded

cattle cars arriving at Auschwitz. As the doctors examined the new arrivals and made selections, it was his job to supervise general registration and property disposal. One line for women and children and another line for men. Turn right or turn left, with a flick of their hand, SS doctors held the fate of the weary and confused waiting for instruction. Left led to death. Right brought reprieve and a chance to live a while longer. Doctors like Mengele who were conducting human experiments, chose first, selecting children, men and women for whatever experiment that caught their fancy under the guise of contributing to the welfare of the greater Reich.

A stream of photographs, documents, and depositions were presented by prosecutors. And then came the witnesses. Elderly children and relatives of the deceased and other survivors, to tell their stories of suffering and horror all within earshot of the old man sitting there in his pressed wool suit. Through tears and curses they pointed him out. If looks could kill . . .

Johann drifted in and out of the parade of accusations that were hurled his way. Of course, his remembrance was one of nuanced regret and shame. He asked himself as he had many times before: "What choice did he have?" Wounded in the battle for France, he could have chosen almost certain death fighting the Russians on the eastern front or accept his assignment to Auschwitz. He chewed on an antacid tablet as he drifted back to his younger self. The rattle and squeal of the trains blended with the sound of doomed Jews and the squeals of their children. And the stench, the never-ending stench of the place itself. No amount of Schnapps could block that out.

He remembered being disoriented when he first arrived at his new post. He had heard about the place where Jews and other undesirables were sent. Still, he was unprepared for the magnitude and scope of the place and the process. Day in and day out, one train after another, soldiers shouting, snarling military dogs, harried intake clerks trying to keep up and of course, men, women and children crying, tormented his efforts at sleep for those first weeks. But then, as unthinkable as it would have been in the world of his youth or in the courtroom where he currently found himself,

Johann began to get used to the chaos and violence. He muttered to himself, "desensitization." That's what the psychologists called it. One becomes desensitized to what would never be acceptable or tolerated in a normal world. He reckoned looking back at those times, the abnormal can easily enough become normal.

When they were finally given the opportunity, his lawyers attempted to point out, in addition to the standard "he was required to follow orders" defense, several other acts of kindness Johann had rendered to camp inmates. Like the time, he noticed one of his former teachers, Herr Steinmenn, being processed. The two of them had often exchanged pleasantries and conversation after one of his lectures. Professor Steinmenn had even sent a letter from his retirement home in Florida verifying that he, Johann Hoffner, had pulled him out of the line destined for the gas chambers and managed to get him assigned to a safe sub-camp that allowed his former teacher to survive the war. There were also several other less notable instances where he had offered a semblance of humane response to inhabitants of Auschwitz. After the war, Johann had learned to be careful and deliberate . . . and patient. Even now, he sat quietly with a kind of resigned stoicism, enduring the evidence and witnesses that discarded the man he had tried to become in favor of the young man that he used to be. He had little doubt that the outcome was predetermined, that he would be extradited to Germany to answer for his alleged war crimes. Nearing ninety, he knew the regrets and secrets he had kept private all these years would now be revealed. No one was interested in the world he had been caught up in. Human survival was after all, a primal instinct that had driven him and others to follow orders—sometimes terrible orders. Since those awful days, Johann had tried to become a better man, to atone in some small way for the unforgivable events he had witnessed and participated in. He had married, raised a family and become a stalwart member of his community and church. He straightened his tie as the final witness took the stand. He had done his best to become his better self. Surely there was some value in that.

Lise Frankel interrupted his reverie. Pointing at him, she demanded, "Johann Hoffner, do you remember me?" Yes, Johann thought to himself. The name did ring a bell, but it was such a long time ago. Ms. Frankel continued. "Now I am an old woman, but I was a young girl then. We lived two houses down from yours on Strasse Street. In summer, I would play in your garden while my mother and your wife would harvest vegetables."

Lise Frankel choked back tears. "When we were being processed at Auschwitz, my mother recognized you. She ran to you. Do you remember how she got down on her knees and begged you to help us? But you didn't, did you Untersturmfuhrer Hoffner? She stood up, her voice rising. Shaking her finger, she shouted, "You slapped her face and kicked her to the ground. You motioned for the guards to put her in the line of death. You sentenced her to death and me to a living death of memories that have robbed me of . . ." Lise Frankel collapsed into her chair, burying her face in her hands, crying for her mother and her lost life.

Johann remembered. He also remembered that Rudolf Hoss, the camp Commandant, was standing nearby. He only listened to the first part of Frau Frankel's comments, tuning out the harshest of her accusations. Instead, he returned to a warm, summer day on Strasse Street. The smell of cooked cabbage, sausages and sauerkraut wafting from the kitchen window made his mouth water. The garden was ready for harvest and flowers were in bloom. Marigolds, chamomile, roses and his favorite, the blue-violet bloom of cornflowers adorned the yard and garden. His wife and her neighbor, Clara, bent over rows of beets, greens and carrots, filling their baskets. He had dug the potatoes a week earlier. He watched a young girl playing in the garden. Her blond hair fell loosely about her face and her blue eyes sparkled as she laughed and danced, singing to herself. She was in a world of her own. He smiled at the thought of it.

Bowing his head, Johann wept.

17

A Small Piece of Blue Sky

"I HAVE SEEN THINGS."

That's all Gerald would say to Dr. Breedlove, his VA psychiatrist.

On the 15th of each month, Gerald's parents, Eugene and Eula Smithwick, dutifully drove their son to Asheville for his appointment at the veteran's hospital. After each session, Dr. Breedlove would talk briefly with them about how he was tweaking this or that medication which he thought might help improve Gerald's condition. He spoke the right words, but his eyes told a different story. They would nod their heads and look at each other. They might be country folks, but country folks possessed better bullshit detectors than most city dwellers, so they soon figured out that the VA Doc was more or less clueless about what to do for their son.

Gerald could usually take care of his basic needs, but most of the time he sat on the back porch, looking out toward the fields. With some coaxing from Eula, he would eat a little at meal-time. Occasionally, he might comment briefly on a past memory, but mostly he would remain silent except when he would whisper, "I have seen things." Sometimes his wounded mantra would be followed by brief sobs. From the vacant look in his eyes and the frozen expression on his face, it was clear to his parents that what he had seen had stopped him in his tracks and put him in some kind of in-between place that was neither here nor there.

Eugene spoke into MacDonald's squawk box. "Two senior coffees, one black, one with cream and one caramel sundae with nuts."

Eula was a frugal woman except when it came to her son and McDonald's caramel sundaes—sometimes she ordered two at the same time. Eugene shook his head at the thought of it.

Merging with traffic on the four-lane bypass around Burnsville, Eugene pointed his trusty old Buick toward home. He sipped his coffee while Eula polished off her sundae and Gerald sat silently in the back seat.

"We been doing this for almost a year now with almost nothing to show for it. What's the point?" Eula looked out the window at the hint of fall's first color. "We do what we can."

"I knew that fourth tour in Iraq was going to get him—I could see it in his eyes. We shouldn't have let him go," Eugene grimaced.

Eula looked at her husband, then glanced at her son in the back seat.

Gerald sat erect with his hands folded in his lap, saying nothing—seeing nothing.

"There were signs," Eugene continued. He had trouble sleeping on his last leave home—and nightmares. He never had them before Iraq."

Eula sipped her coffee. "You should have told them to put two creams in instead of one. His unit was ordered up. What choice did he—we—have?"

Gripping the steering wheel with both hands, Eugene gave his wife a sideways glance. "There's always a choice."

"Maybe the new medicine will. . ." Eula's voice trailed off.

"Medicine my ass," Eugene grunted. "Gerald needs something a pill can't fix."

"Likewhat?"

Eugene relaxed his grip on the steering wheel. "Not sure, but I did hear about a healer up on Humpback Mountain. Goes by the name of Lester McCready."

"A healer? My Lord, Eugene, you've got to be kidding."

Eugene's brow furrowed. "You got any better ideas?"

Eula folded her arms across her chest. "I feel a migraine coming on."

The Buick bucked and rattled its way along the dirt lane that passed for a road in the backwoods of Hump Mountain.

"I don't have a good feeling about this," Eula observed.

Pulling their sedan to a stop, Eugene announced, "This is it."

Sitting on the front porch of a small house that was little more than a shack sat Lester McCready on a church pew that had seen better days. As far as the eye could tell, he was a thin stick of a man. His long white beard mixed with a bit of gray moved gently with the breeze. He wore a faded Green Bay Packers sweatshirt over his work pants. An Atlanta Braves baseball cap perched at an angle on his head. Lester McCready's gray-green eyes followed the three people walking toward him.

Eugene walked ahead and stopped a few feet from the front porch. "Howdy. Are you Mr. McReady, the healer?"

"Name's Lester. And who might you be?"

"My name's Eugene and this here is my wife, Eula and my son, Gerald," Eugene replied. "Some folks down in Bakersville told me how to get here—that you were a healer. Royce Laney down at Kim's Diner called you "the Jesus Man.""

"Like I said, Eugene, my name's Lester."

Eugene glanced uneasily at his wife. "Well, Lester, I got to tell you up front, we ain't believers—I mean as Christians and such. We don't to church except for weddings and funerals. So, to be honest with you, we aren't reliable in the Christianity department."

Lester smiled. "Then you'd probably fit right in with many of my Christian friends. St Francis preached to the birds which I expect were a lot more reliable than his human flock."

Lester looked at Gerald. "I see your son has a troubled spirit."

Gene put his arm around his son's shoulder. "Can you help him?"

"Don't know. Maybe, maybe not. I can give it a try. Why don't the two of you take a walk down through the apple orchard for an hour or so while me and Gerald get acquainted."

When Gerald's parents disappeared around the barn on their way to the orchard Lester took off his cap and pulled his chair up close to Gerald's. Sitting knee to knee, he took Gerald's hands in his hands. Lester could feel Gerald tense up at his touch.

"That's alright, son. You've been through a lot. We'll just sit here and rest a spell."

Lester sat with his eyes closed, holding Gerald's hand for the better part of a half hour. From time to time, he would exhale a soft, low moan.

Opening his eyes, Lester leaned toward Gerald who offered him a passing glance out of the corner of his eye.

"I've seen things."

"Yes, you have son. Yes, you have," Lester replied, patting the young man's hand. "You've been traveling down the low road of sorrow for some time now. You saw behind a curtain you didn't want to pull back and found yourself buried in the quicksand of regret."

A thin bead of perspiration broke out on Lester's forehead as he continued. "All you see are dark clouds and the unspeakable that's hiding behind them. You feel lost in that dark and fearful place where the light can't get through. Those storm clouds of suffering have carried you away from the memory of the blue sky that remains. I'm going to do my best to help you find a small piece of blue sky—just enough blue in the middle of the storm that surrounds you to remember how to find your way back. You won't be alone. I'm going to walk with you. Yesiree, we're going to do it together."

Lester squeezed Gerald's hand gently. "I'm going to pray myself into the middle of your sadness so me and you can go looking for that piece of blue sky."

Lester placed his right hand on Gerald's heart and his left on the back of Gerald's head. Forehead to forehead, Lester began to pray in a kind of whispering silence. As his intercession for Gerald intensified, he and Gerald began to slowly rock back and forth.

Then Gerald began to cry. A long, low moan began coming out of him, starting low in his gut, snaking its way up through every cell in his body. Opening his mouth, Gerald exhaled a prolonged howl that was more animal than human—a sound like no other Lester had ever heard—a sound that ended in the quiet scream of a baby's cry. Gerald collapsed in Lester's arms.

Eugene and Eula walked hand in hand up the pathway from the orchard. The knot in their stomachs gave testimony to the question they waited for an answer to. Rounding the corner of the barn, they saw Lester and Gerald sitting on the front porch sipping coffee. Eula could feel tears welling up in her eyes. Her son was looking "at" her—seeing her. She squeezed her husband's hand.

She spoke his name. "Gerald"

Her son looked at his mother and father and said, "I have seen things."

Eugene looked at his wife, then his son. "You have?"

Gerald nodded. "I have seen blue sky."

After walking his wife and son to the car, Eugene returned to the front porch where Lester stood. He was not a man given to easy expressions of affection, but he couldn't help himself. He embraced Lester. Releasing the old man, he took out his wallet.

Raising the palm of his hand, Lester refused payment. "Blue skies are the breath of heaven. How could a man take payment for that?"

18

Sarah Salvation

LIKE A COCKROACH SEDUCED by a bug light, Francis Quiet Moon shuffled to the edge of an unmarked street corner and stared into the flickering pulse of a streetlamp. A frayed, mustard-yellow knit cap nearly swallowed his head and his tired frame ached from behind the stained, gas-station-attendant's shirt he was wearing. A tattered American flag was tied around his waist—some of the stars had been filled in by different colored crayons, courtesy of his two sons who lived with their mother. His feet were decorated by red and green bowling shoes two sizes too big.

With the remains of his existence stuffed into his Vietnam is-sue duffel bag, Francis had hitchhiked, but mostly walked, his way through the last 100 miles of hill country, traveling the cracked back of a stubborn two-lane that twisted and curled around the Carolina mountains like a serpent. When he walked, the dog tags around his neck clinked like the teeth of a chattering skull. The sound made Francis uncomfortable and he thought about how something as insignificant as two pieces of metal hitting each other could bring back so many bad memories—before and after the war. At one time, Francis had built wind chimes in the cramped basement of the garage apartment he rented with his wife. He couldn't stand the sound of them anymore. They made his head hurt and his heart ache. At night, he would try to force those memories away, make them set with the sun. But every morning they would rise again, burning into his back as he walked, never letting him forget.

He had been losing his grip on sobriety since dawn and had to concentrate just to keep his balance. Francis cringed as the sounds of a honky-tonk version of Sinatra's "My Way" crackled from a nearby convenience store. Picking at the loose threads of his toboggan, he retrieved a near-empty bottle of "Cisco" brand liquor from beneath the remnants of Old Glory. He would often, as he described it, "Disco with Cisco," referring to the bottle as his faithful friend, "Fran-Cisco." The bottle spilled the truth to Francis in a numbing language he could understand. It never cheated on him, never lied to him, or blamed him for a failed marriage. It never confronted him with his past or promised him a future. Although "Fran-Cisco" had been his best friend since a rehab stint after the war, the relationship was stormy. But at least it was his. At least, he could depend on it.

He closed his eyes, took two quick, punishing gulps and gritted his teeth. Peeling open his left eye to squint, Francis could barely make out the lettering of a neon-crimson sign that spelled *Crystal Grape Diner.* Lured by the aroma of food, he slowly gathered up his road-weary carcass and stumbled across the intersection.

Francis stepped inside the diner and slid into a tattered, lime green booth patched by gray duct tape. Sounds from a Crosby, Stills, Nash & Young forty-five wafted from an elaborate jukebox squatting in a smoky corner of the diner like some kind of mechanized Sumo wrestler. Francis' hollow eyes scanned the surroundings for signs of activity while his fingers fumbled with a half-empty pack of Marlboro Lights. He thought about how he used to never smoke. His wife hated it.

Settling on a smoke that seemed dry enough to ignite, Francis lit up. Inhaling deeply, he ran his hands through his hair and observed the other examples of aimless humanity around him. An elderly man in a wheelchair, hooked up to an oxygen tank and dressed in a threadbare tuxedo, played solitaire at one booth. He would light a fresh cigarette every few minutes and let it burn on the edge of an ashtray; never smoking it, just letting it burn.

Francis' eyes followed a succession of Elvis paintings to the other side of the room where a small ruckus was erupting. He extinguished his cigarette on a small tin ashtray and peered through the smoke. A young woman, dressed in a checkered apron and combat boots, was juggling steak sauce bottles, three and four at a time to the cackling delight of four elderly, drunken La-Z-Boy warriors. After finishing her performance, the waitress took a modest bow, laid the party's check on the table and disappeared into the kitchen.

The old men applauded her and were still snorting with laughter as they began to eat their food.

Francis was about to light up another Marlboro when he caught the scent of a pleasant fragrance. A smudged menu slid gently across his knuckles as he lit the cigarette and looked up. Smiling lips asked to take his order. Francis looked above the lips, into eyes warm and dark—shimmering as if fireflies were trapped inside. The tag artfully stitched onto her shirt said "Sarah." She glanced at his duffel bag while fumbling in her pocket for a pen.

"Where ya headed?" she inquired.

"Home," Francis replied in a raspy voice brought on by the late autumn cold.

"Where's home?"

"Don't know yet," he answered, grinning and rubbing his head.

She smiled to herself and nodded while pulling out her pad and pencil to take his order.

"What are your specials tonight?" Francis mumbled.

"Honey, everything I make is special."

Francis drew deeply from his cigarette and grinned so wide his face hurt.

"Well, how about a special cheeseburger and some special fries?" The woman chuckled while taking down his order.

"You're pretty good with those bottles," he added, putting out another cigarette.

"Oh, yeah," she said, laughing. "Well, the way I see it, everybody has a special talent and I guess juggling Heinz 57 bottles for the enjoyment of my red-eyed regulars is mine."

"Aren't you afraid of dropping one of those bottles on someone's head or something?" Francis inquired, rubbing his chapped nose. "You know, with all the lawsuits these days, and what not?"

She smiled and took the menu from his trembling fingers.

"Sometimes you gotta do something risky to make sure you're still alive," she whispered. "Something special, coming up."

She smiled at Francis and clomped off in her combat boots toward the kitchen.

Francis laughed to himself and shook his head in amazement.

Taking a last draw from his cigarette, he looked out the window and watched a couple of young boys in the shadows across the street, kicking an old cardboard box around. He wondered what their names were. His head began to hurt.

He wondered what his own boys were doing, what they had for dinner, what they dreamed about. Francis wondered if they wondered about him. Lighting another cigarette, he thought about how his boys used to always be in his dreams. These visions were like mirrors stitched on his heart, reflecting a time long since passed. The last dream he had was like something out of a movie. It involved a big spread of blue sky that looked like a movie screen in the middle of a dark space. One arm, with the palm open, came in from one side of the sky and another arm, a boy's, came reaching across from the other side of the sky. Both arms were wrapped in barbed wire and reached for each other. That was all Francis could remember. He didn't know what it meant and hesitated to think about it too much, but it haunted him.

Francis finished his meal, laid a few wrinkled bills on the table, and hauled himself and his bag back out into the cold. A crushed velvet night covered him and he stared into its million eyes—"God's peepholes," as his grandmother once called them. The frigid night air filled his lungs and he turned toward the *Crystal Grape*, lighting another cigarette. The half-lit neon sign whirred and popped, making the little shambled building stand out in the shadows like a kind of beacon. A faded "Help Wanted" sign rattled against a storm window.

"Sometimes you have to do something risky to make sure you're still alive." Sarah's words rolled around in what was left of Francis' pinball mind. He stood in the quiet moonlight and looked down the desolate stretch of road that brought him to this place. Putting out his cigarette, Francis turned his head and walked back inside.

19

Midnight at the "Healing Touch"

THE NEON "OPEN" SIGN flickered out as Madge O'Doherty turned to Nadine and Tiffany.

"Tonight was a long one—longer than usual. I could use a drink about now. How about you two?"

Nadine stretched and rubbed the back of her neck. "How about two or three?"

"How about the whole bottle?" Tiffany replied with a laugh.

Looking at the card table set up in the right corner of the waiting room of "The Healing Touch Day Spa", Madge commented to her compatriots, "Looks like the wives left us a nice spread. Chips and dip, a plate of wings, and a baking tin of brownies."

Nadine held up a bottle. "No rot-gut wine tonight. You've moved us up to a fine blue-collar bottle of Yellow Tail."

Madge laughed. "One of the wives left it for us. I think it was Devin's wife, Melissa. Anyway, we earned it. It was a full house tonight."

The three women pulled their chairs around the table, and after pouring the Merlot, settled down to plates of potato chips, French-onion dip, barbeque wings and brownies.

It had indeed, been a long night. For the last six months, one night a week after the regular workday was finished, Madge,

Nadine and Tiffany gave massages to war veterans suffering from PTSD and other ailments.

It started the day Madge overheard two of the wives talking in the checkout line at Food City about how they were at their wit's end with their husbands' drinking, insomnia, nightmares and depression. As it turned out, one of the women, Jenny, was parked next to Madge unloading groceries. After a brief introduction, Madge got to the point: "Jenny, I can't rightly explain what I'm going to offer you, but maybe it has something to do with my best friend's cousin taking his life after he returned from Afghanistan. I can't say for sure. But listening to you and your friends inside, I got this strange kind of urge that I needed to do something. So, I'm offering to work out an arrangement for you and your friends to bring in your husbands one night a week for a therapeutic massage. Maybe it could help them sleep or feel more relaxed. Maybe not. But I am willing to . . ."

Jenny studied Madge's face, looking for an angle. "We're pretty strapped for cash. How much would it cost?"

"Not the regular rate. Whatever you can afford," Madge replied.

That's how it started. One night a week, five thirty 'til whoever showed up was taken care of. After six months, a strange kind of community emerged. While their husbands were getting worked on by Madge, Nadine, and Tiffany, Jenny and her friends formed their own kind of support group. First it was brownies, cookies, pie and coffee. Within the month coffee was replaced by wine, chips and dip . . . and a cup of Joe for the drive home. Jenny always made sure there was food and wine left for the "Healing Touch" team to unwind with after they left.

At first, most of the husbands were reluctant to participate and one, Missy's, dropped out after the second session. And there was Mary Lou's fiancée, Ted, who was banished for pointing to his apparent erection under the sheet and saying to Tiffany, "Why don't you massage that?" The rest of the men settled into the routine, receiving deep tissue, trigger point, shiatsu and Swedish massages while Jenny and the girls caught up with each other in the lounge.

Nadine refilled her tumbler with Merlot. "Girls, this has been quite a ride. Sometimes I can't tell whether I'm a massage therapist, a counselor or a priest."

Dipping a kettle chip into the French onion dip, Madge smiled. "Sometimes we're all three."

Tiffany nibbled on a brownie. "Tonight, Teri's husband, Bert, started sobbing. He apologized, but I told him it was okay—that shiatsu often resulted in clients crying."

"Of course, that's not exactly true," Madge replied, reaching for another chip.

Nadine turned up her wine glass and smacked her lips. "So what? We're just getting a taste of what these guys have been through, and it can get more than a little dark. We're massage therapists, not psychotherapists. I once took a class at the community college that taught us there is a fine line between mind and body."

"Maybe we're a little bit psychotherapist and a whole lot massage therapist," Tiffany added.

"Or maybe we're more like "pyscho-massage therapists," Nadine chimed in.

Madge raised her glass. "I'll drink to that—the three 'pyscho-massage therapists.'"

The three women raised their glasses and drank.

Nadine lit a cigarette. "You know I'm mighty young to be a grandmother. "

"Not that young," Madge added with a chuckle.

"I'm glad to help, but these boys are getting to me," Nadine continued. "I've even started smoking again. Ralph and Jewel didn't show up this week, but last week he told me about how when he was a Tank Commander in Iraq and went through villages they had overrun, there would be dead and burned bodies lying in the streets."

Tiffany put down her half-eaten brownie. "Don't they train them for that sort of thing?"

Nadine blew a smoke ring. "I'm sure they do, but I guess such things can still get to you. Ralph told me about the same nightmare he keeps having. He rounds a corner in a village they have just taken and there are the heads of three dead children lying in the street—looking at him. It's just their heads, but their eyes are blinking and their lips are moving. He's not sure, but he thinks they are whispering 'Why?'"

Stubbing out her cigarette, she looked at Madge and Tiffany, and shook her head. "He began to sweat and his right hand began to tremble. I had him get back on the table, and worked on him for another thirty minutes in order to calm him down."

"And there was poor Jerry who lost both his legs," Tiffany said, looking down at her hands. "He told me there were days he woke up and could still feel them . . . until he looked down and saw they were gone. He never cried out loud, but I could see him wipe his eyes when he didn't think I was looking. The last thing he said to me before he and Priscilla moved in with her parents in Louisiana, was that he never imagined not being able to do for himself."

The three women grew quiet.

Finally, Madge broke the silence. "I haven't mentioned it to you two, but I worked Jenny in for a session last week while Ned was at work. They are having a pretty rough time of it."

Madge poured the three of them the last of the Merlot.

Nadine lit another cigarette. "Tell Jenny next week she needs to bring a bigger bottle of vino—better yet, Jack Daniels. If we're going to work on their guys until midnight, we're gonna need more incentive, 'cause we're definitely not getting any overtime pay."

"Not even minimum wage," Tiffany added.

Madge looked at her two friends. "I don't say it often enough, but I couldn't do this without you two. I know when all's said and done, working on these men doesn't amount to much more than gas money."

"I . . ." she started to continue.

Nadine interrupted her in mid-sentence. "Good Lord, Madge. You know we aren't doing this for the money. We're doing it for these veterans and their poor wives and children. We can damn well sacrifice one night a week after what they and their families have been through."

"I know, I know," Madge responded.

Folding her hands in her lap, Tiffany spoke up. "I'm here for my cousin, Jarvis, who didn't make it back from the first Iraq war. I can still hear him laugh. He had the best kind of laugh. From down deep in his belly, the kind that could fill a room and make people smile just hearing it."

Once more silence, each woman lost in her thoughts.

Finally, Madge sighed. "Ladies, it's time to turn out the lights. Tonight, this party's over."

Nadine stubbed out her cigarette and massaged her left hand with her right. "I believe these here hands have lost their healing touch. They are all healed out."

Tiffany rose from her chair and began collecting the trash from their night's labor. "Tell you what, Granny. I'll work for you tomorrow so you can rest those hands for the weekend."

"Much appreciated, Tiff. In that case, I'll have a nightcap with ol' Jack when I get home—and I don't mean my husband, Jack."

Madge reached out to Nadine and Tiffany. "Group hug?"

Wrapping their arms around each other, they rocked back and forth and replied in unison, "Group hug."

20

The Reunion

SAMMY'S RIB SHACK AND *Resort*—that's what the dented flickering red neon sign said next to the graveled dirt road in front of Sammy's barbeque joint. The building was a mixed bag, the original part an old town shanty and the new edition, a log cabin of sorts. On Saturday nights the parking lot was full. Ford, Chevy and Dodge pick-ups that had seen better days found their perch next to a Mercedes here and a BMW there, along with a mix of Lexus and Cadillac sedans and SUVs. Ever since the Rib Shack had made the *Garden and Gun's* top five southern barbeque eateries, the weekend clientele had moved up a notch or two. The well-heeled Charlotte, Raleigh and Asheville crowd traveled the interstate and backroads to get a taste of Sammy's legendary smoked ribs, sauced or dry-rubbed. That and taking selfies in front of Sammy's bigger-than-life telltale sign.

Inside, a sawdust floor and a pantheon of aromas greeted customers. Along with baby back and beef ribs, smoked pulled pork, beef brisket, chicken, and thick-cut skillet fried potatoes the menu also included vinegar-based coleslaw, slow-cooked pinto and black beans and Brunswick stew. The unlikely star on the chalkboard was M.L.'s hushpuppies, a mix of cornmeal, chopped onions, peppers, and sweet pickles deep-fried into a greasy, golden brown crunch the size of a cat's head biscuit. Some of the regulars were known to order a basket or two to munch on while they downed their happy hour dollar PBRs. Mutt LeDoux, the manager, kept a Louisville Slugger next to the cash register for the late-night brouhahas though rare, that did occur from time to time between locals who had imbibed too much beer and whiskey, and took offense at real or imagined insults from city folks.

Out back near the smokehouse, four middle-aged men sat around a fire pit. A well-seasoned boom box belted out cassette tape classics of their time together—"Fortunate Son" by Creedence Clearwater, The Animal's "We Gotta Get Out of this Place" along with some Otis Redding, Aretha and Smokey Robinson. And to keep Wiley and Big Bob happy, Bobby Bare's "Detroit City" and Porter Waggoner singing "The Green, Green Grass of Home" rounded out the playlist.

Wiley Longfellow stretched his legs from the log he was sitting on, warming his feet near the flaming embers. Wiley was short and wiry, a long-haul truck driver out of Atlanta or "Hotlanta" as he liked to call it. Divorced twice, he no longer drank whiskey, instead sticking to sweet tea. He liked to say, "Me and whisky's mighty risky." One or two drinks and he was up for a fight, usually with someone twice his size that never ended well.

Tall and tan, Townsend Pickens—Towns to his friends, sat in a camp chair and sipped single malt scotch. A lawyer like his father before him, he didn't practice much these days, preferring to oversee the businesses his family had acquired in Charleston. After an overextended courtship, Eleanor "Ellie" Ratliff finally read him the riot act. Six months later they were married on her mother's close friend's plantation.

An aluminum chair creaked under the shifting weight of "Big Bob" Purvis as he leaned over to pull another PBR from the ice chest. Bob was his God-given name, but he had been "Big Bob" since he was twelve, towering two heads above all the other boys. Folks in Funston still talked about the time when two-hundred-pound Big Bob played midget league football. He was quite a sight, plodding toward the opponent's goal line with the football and four or five of the other team's players hanging on him like flies on potato salad at a covered dish church picnic. Big Bob was easy going unless someone pushed him too far. His metal roofing business had kept him, Myrtle and their three kids in good stead.

Finally, there was the host, Sam Brown, creator and owner of *Sammy's Rib Shack and Resort*, the youngest of Midi Lee's twelve children. Hard working, and a natural salesman, he was also good with figures. An ordained minister, he filled the pulpit from time to time at the Ebenezer Baptist Church. After the war, he took care of his Momma and her three youngest, baptizing two of them in Tallahatchee Creek. Sam was fond of saying on occasion, "Corinne and Esther are now members of the 'heavenly choir,' but Ezra's still playing in the Devil's band." Twice engaged, he had never married.

Four middle-aged men from different walks of life sat around the fire pit—three white and one black—brothers of a sort, born and raised together in one mother of a war in a corner of southeast Asia.

Each year since the war ended, they met and reminisced, ever mindful of their brother who was not there, represented by an empty metal folding chair spray painted with the letters *JT*.

Big Bob raised his bottle of beer. "To J.T."

The other three raised their glasses and echoed, "To J.T."

The men sat in silence for a spell, watching the fire pop and crackle the language of remembering.

Wiley poked at an ember with a stick. "J.T. saved my ass more than once. One time when we were on patrol in the Quang Tri province and again during the Tet offensive. A Viet Cong sniper caught me in the side. More blood than real damage. Next thing I knew, there was J.T. flipping me over his shoulder—hell, I was bigger than he was—and carrying me out of harm's way. Then he made his way back to the firefight and took out the sniper for good measure."

Big Bob finished his beer and reached for another PBR. "That boy had some kind of sixth sense when it came to snipers. It was like he had Xray vision. None of the rest of us could see anything, but he could."

"Sixth sense is about right," Towns replied, pouring himself another Scotch. "When it came to war and combat, J.T. had a sixth sense about everything."

Wiley refilled his glass of tea. "He was like a mother hen and we were his chicks."

Sam opened a bottle of bourbon and poured two fingers of whiskey into his coffee cup.

"Sammy, I figured you were done with whiskey, you being a Reverend and all," Wiley grinned.

Taking a sip, Sam smacked his lips. "Wiley, old buddy, I only drink whiskey once a year when we get together. We drank a lot of it in 'Nam . . . and we smoked a lot of weed. I don't smoke weed, but I will drink a bit of bourbon in remembrance. Also, because when our reunion time is over and we go our separate ways, I tend to get a bad case of the night sweats."

Wiley nodded and gave his friend a salute of understanding.

Towns got up and threw another log on the fire. He looked at his brothers in arms.

"J.T. saved us, but he couldn't save himself."

"Even worse, he couldn't save himself from himself," Sam interjected, shaking his head.

"I remember how he began to change. Most of us did what we had to do, but we also tried to stay alive. After Tet, J.T. started volunteering to be point on patrols, putting himself in the line of fire when he didn't have to."

Big Bob shifted in his chair. "We were always tired and on edge. I don't think I ever had a good night's sleep the whole time I was there. I can remember waking up one night after a bad dream and there was J.T. sitting by the fire cleaning his weapon and sharpening the hunting knife he carried. He looked at me and winked."

Towns reached for his bottle of Scotch. "I remember the change. We would all be sweating patrol and J.T. would be in the lead, calm as a cucumber . . . sometimes even smiling or at least, it looked like he was to me."

Sam lit his pipe. "Fellas, after the war, I've prayed for J.T and the rest of you bozos as well. Even though I don't clearly understand it, Brother J.T. crossed some sort of line. He seemed to me to have a kind of gleam in his eye . . . like he was going hunting . . . like he was keeping score of his kills."

The men grew quiet again.

Wiley folded his hands and stared at the fire. "When we shipped out from Danang, he reupped. It didn't make sense. It was toward the end of our tour and the writing was on the wall. Most folks were trying to keep their head down and survive. Hell, those boys in Troop B—the entire company refused to carry out the operation they were ordered to do."

"Search and destroy became search and avoid," Big Bob mumbled.

Towns looked out toward the woods. "Lots of drugs—weed and heroin . . . and booze were going down. You could smell defeat behind all Westmoreland's and McNamara's lying bullshit about casualties and how we were winning. And those poor spit and polish lieutenants fresh out of ROTC and West Point . . . if they didn't have a good sergeant or if they didn't listen to him, they weren't long for this world."

Popping the top off another beer, Big Bob took a long draw. "Yep. For awhile near the end, there seemed to be a "fragging" almost every week or else a lieutenant missing in action. The smart ones listened and learned."

"And lived," Wiley replied.

Towns lit a cigar. "In spite all of that. In spite of everything going to hell in a handbasket. When we said our goodbyes, no matter what we said or promised or how hard we tried to talk him out of it, J.T. still reupped."

"I hate to say it, but maybe it was for the best," Sam said. "After our brother went through the change, I've thought more than once that he wouldn't have made it in the world we returned to."

"A lot of folks don't," Towns replied. "I've been doing some pro bono work down at the prison for veterans. There's a dozen or more doing time for something that was okay to do in 'Nam. Everybody was smoking weed or hashish. No problem there, but here first-time offenders are getting a year for each joint they are caught with. The prison counselor and Warden say they don't belong in prison, but the local battle axe of a judge and the politicians running for re-election don't agree."

Big Bob finished off his fourth PBR and spit into the fire. "Welcome home soldiers and thank you for your service."

"That's right. Welcome, home," Sam echoed. "Course I doubt J.T. would have fit in prison either. Bad enough the reception we got from some folks when we returned home."

Wiley stared at the fire. "Yeah, the world we returned to was something else. I still remember being called 'Baby Killer'. When I walked off the plane some long-haired hippy of a girl with flowers in her hair, holding a peace sign, spit at me. You may be right, Sammy, about J.T. not being able to fit in. Can you imagine what he would have done to her?"

Sam chuckled at the thought of it. "She'd a been wearing that sign in a place where the sun don't shine. Then again, maybe that makes my point. How in the world would J.T. have been able to adjust to what we came back to?"

Big Bob leaned forward and placed his hands on his knees. "I know you're probably right, but I sure do miss him. And I wish he had come with us."

Sam looked at the night sky. "Amen to that, Big Bob."

And they all said together, "Amen to that."

www.ingramcontent.com/pod-product-compliance
Lightning Source LLC
Chambersburg PA
CBHW060125260626
47160CB00005B/2022